MW00466354

# PROTECTING KIERA

## A SEAL OF PROTECTION NOVELLA

SUSAN STOKER

# CHAPTER 1

KIERA HAMILTON STOOD in a corner of *My Sister's Closet*, the secondhand clothing store owned by her friend, Julie Hurt, and sipped the lukewarm champagne she'd been nursing for most of the night.

She'd only agreed to attend the shindig because Julie had let it slip that Cooper would be there.

Cooper Nelson. The man was six feet, two inches of perfection, and way out of her league. Not only that, he was too young for her. There were a million other reasons why it was stupid for Kiera to have a schoolgirl crush on the man, but it hadn't prevented her from going out of her way to attend the small party.

Kiera had met Julie when her first-grade class had toured the Navy base. Julie had been there visiting her husband, and when one of the children in the class had wet his pants, she'd come to the rescue. Her car had been full of clothes she'd just picked up from the cleaners to take to her store to sell, and she just happened to have a couple pairs of little boy pants. They'd hit it off, and now spent most of their free time together.

Kiera knew all about Julie's past...how she was the daughter of a senator who'd been kidnapped a few years ago. Julie had been upfront about how awful she'd been to her rescuers during that ordeal, and how she now felt like she'd finally found the person she was meant to be.

She owned and operated the small boutique, selling used designer clothes. She also donated a healthy amount of her inventory to homeless women who needed nice outfits to interview in, lower-income girls who needed dresses to wear to high school dances, and lately, she'd even begun selling men's clothing, as well as donating Armani and other designer suits to down-on-their-luck men who needed to make a good impression.

"Are you having a good time?"

Kiera startled and almost dropped the flute of champagne, but managed to keep hold of it. She turned with a smile to Julie. "Of course. You must be thrilled at the turnout tonight."

Julie's smile was huge as she nodded. "Sometimes I have to pinch myself at how well things have worked out. Not only did I find the man of my dreams, but I've actually been able to make a difference in many people's lives. It feels good."

Kiera beamed at her friend. Tonight's celebration came about because a young woman who Julie had given a professional outfit to a few years ago was interviewed by a local television station in Los Angeles, and the story had subsequently gone national. The woman's story, unfortunately, wasn't unusual. She'd escaped an abusive relationship, had gotten into drugs and was living on the streets. She'd cleaned herself up enough to get into a homeless shelter, but couldn't find a job.

Julie had met her in her first year of business, during one of her trips to the shelter to talk to the women who ran it. She'd invited Rebecca, the woman looking for a job, to her shop to pick out an outfit free of charge. To make a long story short, Rebecca had gotten the job she'd interviewed for and now, two short years later, had made her way up to an executive manager position.

The party tonight was more to celebrate Rebecca's success than anything else, but the influx of donations, both monetary and clothing, was a boon to rejoice in as well.

Kiera looked around, noting there were quite a few of Riverton's elite at the party. The mayor was there with his wife and she recognized the Chief of Police as well. As her gaze swung around the room, she stopped on Cooper and sighed. She had it so bad for him.

Cooper had been under Julie's husband's command as a Navy SEAL, but was injured while on a mission and had retired. An explosion had gone off too close to where he'd been standing, and while he'd gotten away with all his limbs, he'd lost hearing in his right ear, and almost seventy percent in his left.

Kiera worked with deaf children at the Riverton School for the Deaf, and had seen Cooper when he'd shown up to volunteer with the children. The first time she'd seen him standing in the hallway of the school, she'd been surprised at the immediate attraction she'd had toward him. She wasn't the kind of woman who fell in lust at first sight, but Cooper just did something for her. He was tall, which she loved. Even though she'd spent her life looking up at people, there was just something about a man towering over her that turned her on. It made her feel more feminine, protected...something.

He had russet-colored eyes that were a shade lighter than his dark brown hair, which was badly in need of a trim. He'd been wearing jeans that molded to his muscular thighs and a short-sleeve polo shirt had shown off his bulging biceps. All in all, he was beautiful and intimidating at the same time.

She was just Kiera. Not a super soldier or really anyone extraordinary. Like a lot of women, she had extra pounds on her slight frame that she couldn't seem to get rid of...not that she'd really tried. After a bad experience with extreme dieting in college, Kiera had decided to try to live a life of moderation, not deprivation. She ate and drank what she wanted, tried to stay fairly active without being a crazy workout freak, and as a result, was content with her body.

But looking at Cooper that day, she'd suddenly wished she spent more time at the gym and hadn't eaten the sleeve of Girl Scout cookies the night before. Amazingly, however, he hadn't seemed bothered by her weight. He'd smiled at her, shook her hand and, unless she was completely misinterpreting the look in his eyes, seemed to be attracted to her.

Since that first meeting, Kiera had spoken to

Cooper every time he'd visited the school. They'd laughed together and she'd thought they were hitting it off. She'd believed their attraction was mutual, but he hadn't done anything about it. She figured that maybe he was reluctant because she worked at the school where he was volunteering, so when Julie said Cooper had promised to come to the party that night, Kiera had jumped at the chance to attend.

But she might as well've stayed home, doing what she usually did on Saturday nights...namely, sitting on her couch either reading or watching TV. Cooper was at the party, but it almost seemed as if he was avoiding her, staying on the far side of the store. Kiera had watched him, and he seemed out of sorts and irritated, not talking to anyone, merely giving chin lifts to the other SEALs who were attending.

Kiera had pretty good self-esteem, she liked her job, loved working with children, and even though she was short, liked her body most days. And she generally didn't mind the fact that she was an intro-vert, preferring to sit at home by herself than go out and hang with friends. But standing in a corner, watching the groups of women laughing together, how the attached men doted on their wives without them seeming to notice, and as Julie's husband,

Patrick, kept glancing over at his wife and smiling, made Cooper's standoffish manner—after she'd thought they were friends—all the more frustrating and depressing.

She was brought out of her musings by Julie's hand on her arm. She'd almost forgotten the other woman was standing next to her and they'd been having a discussion about how she'd gotten together with her husband. "You've totally made a difference in Riverton. You should be proud of yourself."

Kiera's gaze swung behind the other woman and she said, "Speaking of the man of your dreams," She got the words out right before Patrick came up behind Julie and put his arm around her waist.

"It's good to see you, Kiera," he said after kissing his wife on the temple.

"You too. All good on base?"

"Can't complain. You talked to Coop tonight?"

Kiera wasn't surprised he'd brought him up. He'd told her, in confidence, that Cooper was having a hard time adjusting to civilian life. He'd planned on being in the Navy for as long as they'd have him...but losing most of his hearing made that time end about twenty years before he was ready.

"No. Our paths haven't crossed," Kiera told him

honestly, not mentioning that it wasn't for lack of effort on her part.

"Damn stubborn sailor," Patrick murmured under his breath.

Kiera's eyes flicked over to the corner Cooper had been occupying almost without her thinking about it. He was still there, frowning and looking extremely tense. She knew Julie was talking, but Kiera barely heard her. Something about Cooper's body language was bugging her. She tilted her head and kept her eyes on him for a long moment.

"...right?" Julie nudged her arm to get her attention.

"I'm sorry...what?" Kiera asked, looking back at Julie apologetically.

"I was just saying that Patrick talked to his secretary and he—"

"Admin assistant," Patrick interrupted.

"What?" Julie asked.

"Admin assistant. Not secretary. I don't think Cutter would enjoy being called a secretary."

Julie rolled her eyes at her husband and smiled at Kiera. "Sorry...Patrick's admin assistant," she brought her hands up and used them to make air quotes around the words, "said he'd gladly arrange another visit if you wanted. He loved hanging out with the kids."

"I don't know, we were quite the intrusion," Kiera said reluctantly. And they had been. Taking kids who couldn't hear on any field trip was never easy, but a trip to a working base with men in uniform and all their toys had been especially interesting with her group. The fourteen kids in her class could hardly contain their excitement, signing in their limited vocabulary and loving the attention they'd received from the sailors.

"Never an intrusion," Patrick said with a smile. "Kids are a gift." His hand moved to Julie's belly and he pulled her back against him, caressing her all the while.

"Oh my God, are you pregnant?" Kiera blurted, eyes wide.

Julie smiled and tilted her head up to Patrick. Her hand came to cover his on her stomach and she nodded.

"Congrats, that's so great!" Kiera gushed.

"Thanks. We're pretty happy," Julie told her friend.

"As well you should be. When are you due?"

"Six months or so. I'm only about twelve weeks along."

"Seriously, that's awesome."

"Yeah. We think so too. Anyway, Coop's been coming to the school, right?" Patrick asked.

Kiera nodded. "I saw him several times last week. We even had lunch one day."

"What's his problem then?" Patrick mused, more to himself than either of the women standing with him. "He's standing over there acting like an asshole. I'm going to tell him to get his head out of his ass or go home."

Patrick shifted behind Julie as if to do exactly that when it finally hit Kiera what was up with Cooper.

"No, don't. Let me talk to him."

Both Patrick and Julie's eyes came to her. "Something I need to know?" Patrick asked in a commanding voice.

Kiera shook her head quickly. "It's just...I think I know why he's been so out of sorts tonight."

"Want to share?" Patrick asked.

Kiera bit her lip in indecision.

"Never mind," Julie's husband said. "I suppose it's not important. If you can get through to him, I'd be grateful. But, Kiera..."

She looked up at the tall, forceful man. She'd more than once had the thought that Julie was a lucky woman after talking with Patrick. He was everything she'd always wanted in a man...and hadn't been able to find. Strong, sure of himself, gentlemanly, and protective.

When she met his gaze, Patrick continued, "If he's not polite to you, let me know. He might not be under my command anymore, but no man disrespects a woman when I'm around. I'll be watching."

Kiera swallowed hard. She knew Julie and Patrick, but they weren't people she would exactly call best friends. But hearing Patrick say he'd have her back felt good. Really good. It had been a long time since anyone had done what Julie's husband was offering...even if she didn't think it was necessary.

"I'll be fine," Kiera reassured Patrick. "Cooper wouldn't do anything like that."

Patrick shrugged. "Maybe the Coop I used to know. But ever since he was injured, I'm not sure."

Kiera started to get upset. Even though Cooper had been ignoring her all night, she didn't think he'd be disrespectful to her face, and still wanted to defend him. "Maybe you don't know him as well as you think you do," Kiera fired back, an angry flush to her cheeks. It was a juvenile come-back, as the man knew Cooper way better than she did, but she couldn't stand there and say nothing.

Patrick didn't respond for a long moment before his lips twitched as if he was suppressing a smile. "Let me know if I can help in any way."

"I will," Kiera forced herself to say. She didn't want to piss off the commander, but jeez. "I'll talk to you later, Julie."

"Later, Kiera," the other woman responded.

Kiera put her champagne glass down on a tray sitting nearby and headed across the room toward Cooper. She couldn't believe it had taken her so long to figure out what his issue was. Now that she had, she kicked herself for not acting sooner.

# CHAPTER 2

Cooper Nelson stood against the wall of the small boutique that belonged to his former commander's wife and stared blankly at the people milling about around him. His head felt like it was going to explode. He glanced down at his watch to see how much longer he had to suffer before he could politely bow out.

He genuinely wanted to be there; he was happy for Julie and Patrick, but the ringing in his ears was excruciating. It was almost ironic that while he'd lost most of his hearing, at the moment he wished he'd lost all of it.

Cooper hadn't thought much about the party and how it would affect him. He'd just gotten in his car and showed up, as he would've before he was injured. But the longer he was there, and the more people filled the small space, he quickly realized that the buzz of voices and low music playing was amplified by his hearing aid. He'd tried turning the volume on the device down, but as a result he'd been unable to hear what anyone said to him when they spoke, so he'd turned it back up. And the fact that the noise was only registering on one side of his head made him feel off kilter, and even a little sick to his stomach.

He'd arrived at the get-together excited to see Julie's friend again, but his excitement had quickly waned when he realized how hard it was to hear, and now he just wanted to go home and hide in his blissfully silent apartment.

Just as he'd decided that it was time to leave, whether or not it was rude, he felt a hand on his arm. Looking down, Cooper saw the reason he was at the party at all standing next to him, her brow furrowed in concern.

Kiera Hamilton.

He'd been fascinated by the woman since the first day he'd met her. Patrick had recommended/ordered he volunteer at a deaf school near the base, and Cooper hadn't been happy about it. He'd felt as if his commander was pushing his disability down his throat and it had pissed him off. He'd gone, but had sworn to himself that he was just doing it the one time to placate Patrick.

The moment Cooper had seen Kiera, he'd been smitten.

Smitten. It was such a silly word for how she made him feel. It didn't matter that she was ten years older than him or that she was way out of his league. The second he saw her signing with a child in the middle of the lunchroom, he'd wanted to get to know her.

He'd seen a lot of dark things in his twenty-seven years, things no human should ever witness, let alone participate in. He'd known it going in. Had known being a Navy SEAL wasn't all glorious Hollywood-style hostage rescues, but the reality had been much harsher than even he could've imagined. Body parts strewn across the sand after a bomb exploded, hostages who had been abused so badly they were mere shells of who they used to be, blood, guts, gore, and the worst of humanity.

He didn't remember much about the explosion that had stolen his hearing...only recalled the horrible pain in his ears and the blood pouring out of them as if a faucet had been turned on high.

But seeing Kiera's smile as they were introduced

had almost made everything he'd seen and done disappear. She was his reward, she just didn't know it yet.

So when Patrick had not-so-subtly told him that Kiera was going to be at his wife's party that night, Cooper had jumped at the chance to talk to her outside of her work. To discuss something other than learning sign language, how his hearing aid was working out, and what he thought about the school lunches he'd been eating with the children.

But his fantasies of chatting with her in a neutral setting disappeared like smoke when Cooper realized that he'd never be able to hear her in the noisy room, and when the pain in his head started.

"Come on," Kiera demanded.

Cooper didn't actually hear the words, but instead read her lips. She surprised the hell out of him when she reached down and intertwined her fingers with his and tugged. Without protest—Kiera could hold his hand anywhere, anytime—Cooper docilely followed behind her.

If his former teammates could see him now, they'd get a kick out of the situation. The woman clutching his hand wouldn't be able to budge him if he didn't want to go with her, but he did. Cooper had no idea where she was taking him, but it didn't matter. He'd follow her to the ends of the earth. The view of her ass in her skirt was merely a bonus. Even though it felt as if there were hundreds of gnomes pounding inside his head with little hammers, he smiled.

As the diminutive woman led them toward the front door of the boutique, Cooper placed the glass of champagne he hadn't been drinking on a table they passed. He noted absently that Kiera waved off at least three people, not stopping to chat, not even to be polite. He appreciated it. He needed fresh air. Badly. Before the nausea swirling deep in his belly got the better of him. He didn't think Julie would appreciate him hurling all over the floor of her shop.

Catching Patrick's eye, Cooper lifted his chin in a goodbye of sorts. In return, the other man flashed him the hand signal for "be careful."

Kiera didn't give him a chance to respond, but Cooper understood Patrick's warning. Kiera was friends with his wife. If he fucked with her, he'd fuck with his former commander. But Cooper had no intention of fucking with Kiera...not in the sense Patrick was warning him about.

Cooper had the quick thought that the hand signals the teams used to talk to each other when they couldn't speak were an awful lot like sign language, but before he could dwell on that more, they were outside the small shop.

The immediate silence of the night was blissful. Even the slight ringing in his left ear was tolerable. Kiera didn't stop, but continued as if she had a specific destination in mind, and Cooper didn't say a word.

She led them past the independently owned businesses that lined the street to Julie's store until they reached a small square. It reminded him of the ones in the rural towns he'd grown up around in the Midwest, all it was missing was a large courthouse. There was a building in the middle of the area—Cooper had no idea what was inside—and around it was green lawn, a fountain off to one side, and a multitude of benches. It was a cozy place where shoppers could come to rest, employees could eat their lunch, or parents could bring their kids to be out in the fresh air instead of cooped up inside.

Kiera led him to a bench and stopped. She pointed down at it and signed the word for sit. Cooper's lips twitched but he did as she ordered.

When they were both seated, she frowned up at him and said slowly, giving him a chance to read her lips in case his ears were still ringing, "When you're in a small, enclosed area with lots of people, you should turn off your hearing aid. All it's gonna do is give you a headache."

She was right.

"You're right." He tried to monitor how loud he was speaking, but couldn't. There were times he knew he was talking way too loud and others when whoever he was speaking to had to ask him to repeat whatever it was he'd said, as he was almost whispering and didn't know it, but Kiera didn't give him any clues if his voice was at an appropriate level or not. She just responded.

"I know."

Cooper couldn't hold back his grin anymore. "How'd you know?"

"That you were in pain?"

He nodded.

"Besides the fact your brows were permanently drawn down, you kept tilting your head to the left as if that would block the sound, you fiddled with your ear several times and you were squinting?"

Cooper's grin left his face. Damn. He'd thought he'd hidden his discomfort better than that. "Yeah, besides that."

Kiera put her hand over his on his leg. The warmth of her touch almost scorched him. He froze, not wanting to move even an inch if it'd mean her removing her hand from his.

"For one, I've seen the kids in my class with partial hearing act exactly the same way you were when the noise is too loud. It took me a bit, as I'm used to watching in the classroom for signs someone's hearing aid is bothering them, not at a party like the one tonight. And secondly, you were being rude. Not talking to anyone. Not even saying hello to me."

"I'm sorry, I—"

"No, don't apologize. I wouldn't talk to anyone either if my ears were ringing and a jackhammer was going off in my brain." She smiled when she said it, and Cooper could see the sincerity in her eyes.

"How do you know what it feels like?"

"I don't. Not really. But I've talked to enough of my students and heard them describe the feeling that I've learned to recognize it. It took me longer with you though."

When she didn't continue, Cooper asked, "Why?"

A slight blush moved up her neck and into her cheeks, giving her a rosy glow. She pulled her hand away from his and clasped them together in her lap. She looked away from him and shrugged.

Cooper put one finger under her chin and gently pulled her back to face him. "Why?" he repeated.

"My feelings were hurt that you didn't seem to want to talk to me," Kiera blurted, then pressed her lips together.

"I'm sorry."

"No, it's fine. It's silly really. I just…I usually stay at home on the weekends. I'm an introvert at heart, and after a week of being with the kids and talking with the other teachers and parents, I'm exhausted. But when Julie told me you were going to be at her party, I thought maybe we could talk away from school." She shrugged, not taking her eyes from his. "Then I got there and you wouldn't even look at me. It hurt. But I understand now. It's not a big deal."

Cooper's stomach tightened, but not from nausea this time. Kiera had wanted to talk to him. She came to the party because he was going to be there. He felt just like he had when he was ten years old and Renee Vanderswart said he could walk her to her bus after school one day. Giddy. Excited.

He put his hand over hers in her lap. "The only reason I was there was because Patrick said you'd be there."

Cooper saw her blue eyes light up. "Really?"

"Yeah," he confirmed. "But by the time I got there,

it was already crowded. The second I walked in the store, my hearing aid started buzzing. I knew I wouldn't be able to have a decent conversation with you, and I was too stubborn and embarrassed to take the stupid thing out and fiddle with it. So I thought I'd stay long enough to be polite and then take off. I'd already decided to explain when I saw you at school in a few days."

"I understand."

"I don't think you do," Cooper countered.

She tilted her head and wrinkled her brow.

"Kiera, I wanted to impress you. But I knew I wouldn't be able to hear myself speak, and I couldn't tell if I was yelling or whispering. Not to mention, I wouldn't be able to hear what you were saying. I'm getting better at reading lips, but I still have a long way to go. And since I'm being honest, I still can't tell if I'm talking too loud or soft, but I can hear you pretty well at the moment, so there's that."

"You're doing fine," she reassured him.

Cooper squeezed her hands. "The point is, I want you to see me as a man, Kiera. Not as a wounded ex-sailor. Not as a student."

She stared at him for a long moment, and Cooper could feel his heart beating hard in his chest. It was ridiculous. He'd stared down the scope on a rifle for hours waiting for the right moment to take his shot and hadn't felt this kind of adrenaline rush.

Kiera took a deep breath, but didn't look away from him. In many ways, she was eons braver than he'd ever been.

"I'm old enough to be your mother."

Cooper stared at her for a beat, then threw his head back and laughed. When he got himself under control, he looked back down at Kiera and chuckled anew. She was glaring up at him with squinty eyes. He ran a fingertip between her eyebrows. "The only way you'd be able to be my mother is if you were sexually active in elementary school, sweetheart."

"You're missing the point," she huffed, trying to pull her hands out from under his. "And how do you know how old I am anyway?"

Cooper got serious. "I'm not missing the point, and I asked Patrick."

She gaped up at him. "You asked Patrick?"

"Yup. He asked his wife, who told him, and he told me. You're thirty-seven. Have been working at the Riverton School for the Deaf for ten years. Your mom is deaf and that's how you learned to sign. You've never been married and haven't dated seriously in at least five years. You met Julie when you took your kids to the base for a tour. She had an extra pair of pants for one of your students when he had an accident."

Kiera gaped up at him.

Cooper smiled, loving having the upper hand. Loving the dance. He'd been pussyfooting around her for long enough. It was time he stopped and let her know how he felt. "Yeah, I asked, Kiera. I wanted to know everything about you."

"Why?"

"You have to ask?"

She dropped her eyes for the first time and the blush returned.

"I want to get to know you. I want to know what you like to eat, about your childhood. I want to meet your parents, but hopefully you can teach me to be more fluent in sign language before we do. I want to be able to talk to your mom and have her tell me stories about what you were like when you were a kid. I want to know what your home looks like, if you can cook, and what you like to watch on TV."

She bit her lip and took a deep breath.

Cooper forced himself to continue. "I want all that stuff, but I know you could do so much better than me. I've seen stuff that would make you reel in horror. Things I don't ever want to think or talk about again. Most of the time I'm uncouth and say the wrong thing. I don't have patience for stupid people and I'm not sure I want to have children. I don't have a college degree and I'm disabled. I'm afraid I won't be able to protect a woman like I should, since I can't hear what's going on around me, and that sucks."

"Cooper—" Kiera began, but he interrupted her, wanting to get it all out.

"I don't give a shit about the ten years between us. I'm twenty-seven, but some days I feel eighty-seven. It's not about the number, it's about this feeling inside me that is screaming you're the reason that bomb didn't rip me to pieces. It should've, Kiera. I was standing right there. I know I sound insane, but I think everything happens for a reason, and the reason I lost my hearing was so I could meet you. All I'm asking for is a chance. Give me a chance to show you I'm not an asshole...well, not to *you*. I swear if you let me into your life, I'll do everything in my power to make your next forty years better than the first."

Cooper stopped talking and could see emotions swirling through Kiera's eyes. He held his breath, waiting for her response.

# CHAPTER 3

KIERA STARED up at Cooper in disbelief. There was so much in what he'd said...she didn't know where to start.

He'd asked about her. Her. Not only asked, but probed.

But one thing stuck out above everything else. "You're not disabled."

He snorted. "I hate to be the one to break this to you, but I am."

Kiera shook her head vehemently. "Gandhi once said, 'Strength does not come from physical capacity. It comes from an indomitable will.' My other favorite quote is by Oscar Pistorius. He's the South African Olympic sprinter who had both legs amputated below the knee when he was a baby."

"I know who he is," Cooper said with a smile. "Wasn't he also convicted of killing his girlfriend?"

"Yes, but that's beside the point. Actually, it probably makes my point more. I bet if he saw himself as disabled he wouldn't have been able to kill anyone. *Anyway*, I was going to tell you something he once said. 'You're not disabled by the disabilities you have, you are able by the abilities you have.'"

"I'm not sure my abilities are things polite society wants or needs," Cooper said dryly.

Kiera moved one of her hands to his leg and said softly, "I teach the children in my classes that they can be whatever they want. They can do whatever they want. They might need to make adjustments to accommodate them, but just because there's never been a deaf opera singer doesn't mean there never will be."

"I bet if I Googled it, I'd find one," Cooper told her.

"You're missing my point," Kiera huffed, sitting back in frustration.

"I'm not, I'm just teasing. I promise to work on my attitude about my loss of hearing, but you'll need to give me some time. I was a SEAL, sweetheart. One of the most feared and respected men in the military. Now I'm out of a job and struggling to figure out what to do with the rest of my life. I can't do many of the things I took for granted and it's…hard."

Kiera had more respect for Cooper at that moment than she did for most other people. He didn't shy away from the fact that he was floundering after retiring from the Navy. She decided to move on and commented on some of the other things he'd said earlier.

"First of all, you're more…male…than most men I've ever met. You being able to hear or not has no bearing on that whatsoever."

His lips didn't move, but the lines around his eyes deepened with her words…as if he was smiling with his eyes. She continued, hoping she'd convinced him on that particular point.

"I don't care if you say the wrong thing at the wrong time. I'm too old to care what others think about me or my friends. Stupid people are one of my pet peeves. And I love kids and being around them all day, but I also love going home to my quiet apartment, putting my feet up, and drinking a glass of wine. I'm not sure at this point in my life I want kids either."

It was the first time she'd said the words out loud and they were somehow freeing. "Society thinks women who don't want to procreate are somehow wacked in the head. But I enjoy my life. I *like* being able to go on vacation wherever and whenever I want. I don't care about your lack of a degree; you're smart, have common sense, and I'd rather be around you than a lot of so-called educated people I know. You don't have to protect me. I've been taking care of myself for a really long time. And if there is something you need to know that you can't hear, I don't mind passing along the intel."

They stared at each other for a long moment.

"Does that mean you're okay with our age difference?" Cooper asked quietly. So softly Kiera could barely hear him.

"Not really," she said honestly. When his brows wrinkled in frustration or disbelief, she wasn't sure which, she hurried to explain. "I'm afraid if we do get together you'll decide in a few years that you've wasted your late twenties. That you'll think you've missed out. I'll be in my late forties when you're still in your thirties. I'll be hitting menopause when you're—"

Cooper stopped her rambling with a hand over her mouth. When she stopped speaking, he moved his hand until his fingertips rested against the back of her neck and his thumb brushed the apple of her cheek.

"If you give me a shot, and we end up together, I'll never, ever, regret a second of our time with each other. I haven't been a monk, but any desire I might've had to take random women home with me died the second that bomb exploded. I didn't have anyone to talk to, to sit by my side as I recuperated… and I realized how much time I'd wasted. I don't want a meaningless hookup. I want a committed relationship with a woman who wants to spend her life with me. Give me a chance, Kiera. A chance to show you that I'm not a fuckup. That I can be the kind of man who'll treat you like you were meant to be treated."

"Promise me one thing," Kiera said.

"Anything."

"That if you change your mind, if the difference in our ages does start to bother you, you do want kids, or if you want more than the boring life of sitting around and watching TV on a Saturday night, you'll tell me. Don't cheat on me, hit me, or do something else so *I* have to break up with *you*."

"I promise," he said immediately. "But I'll tell you right now, it's never gonna happen. First, I'd be an idiot to cheat on you. I know for a fact that we're gonna be combustible in bed together. Sitting here holding your hand has me more excited and aroused than I've ever been before. I have no doubt you're gonna blow my mind if we ever make love. And after the last few years on the teams, I can't think of anything better than hanging out with you every night doing nothing. I've had enough excitement to last me a lifetime. And there's no way in hell I'd ever hurt you. No way."

"But if—"

"No ifs, ands, or buts about it, sweetheart. But if it makes you feel better, yes, I promise I'll tell you straight up if I don't think things are working out between us, so we can both move on with no hard feelings."

Kiera sighed in relief, then nodded.

They stared at each other for a long moment before she asked, "How's your head?"

"Better."

She brought her hand up to his face and mirrored his hand placement, brushing her thumb against his cheek. "So...now what?"

"A kiss to seal the deal?"

Her lips twitched. "To *SEAL* the deal?"

He grinned. "Yeah."

"I'd like that."

Cooper's head moved toward hers and Kiera held her breath. If asked, she never would've guessed this was how the night would've ended, especially not after seeing Cooper standing in a corner, his shields up, rebuffing anyone who tried to come near him.

Kiera closed her eyes and the second their bodies made contact, she swore she saw stars. His lips brushed hers tentatively once, then with more confidence a second time. Kiera tightened her grip on his neck and pulled him into her, telling him without words how much she liked his touch.

When Cooper's tongue swiped along her bottom lip, she gasped, giving him the opening he'd obviously been waiting for. He used his hold on her to tilt her head to a better angle and he wasted no time delving inside her mouth.

He used his tongue as well as she imagined he handled a weapon—with pinpoint accuracy and confidence. He knew what he was doing...and Kiera could only hang on for the ride. He alternated between forceful thrusts, which mimicked what she so desperately wanted him to do to her body at a later date, and easy, soft caresses.

After several moments, he pulled back and nuzzled her nose with his own. Kiera opened her eyes and blinked up at him, licking her lips, tasting him on them. "So...now what?" she repeated.

Cooper smiled. "Now what? We date. Get to

know each other. Flirt at your workplace. Steal kisses. You'll continue to teach me to sign and I'll treat you like you're the most important thing in my life."

"I have a feeling you're not going to have any issues picking up sign language, if the last couple of weeks have been any indication," Kiera told him. She'd been impressed with how quickly he'd been able to learn the basics, and knew with more time spent on it, he'd quickly become proficient.

Cooper leaned forward, kissed her once more—a closed-mouth kiss that still made her knees weak—and stood. "I have a good teacher. Come on, I'll walk you to your car."

With a smile, Kiera stood and they walked hand in hand to the parking lot.

*  *  *

The next morning, Cooper walked through the building he used to call his home at the Navy base. He nodded at some of the SEALs who were hanging around. He'd gotten to know some of them a lot better since his injury. He'd been afraid after he was medically retired that he'd never again have the kind of camaraderie he'd come to rely on from his team, but the men, and sometimes their wives, had been there throughout his recovery. They'd brought food, come to visit, and encouraged him to work out with them in the mornings.

A man with salt and pepper hair and a neatly trimmed mustache and beard, a former SEAL himself, sat at a desk outside Patrick Hurt's office and lifted his chin as Cooper came toward him.

"Hey, Coop. Lookin' good."

"Thanks, Cutter. How're things?"

"Can't complain," Slade "Cutter" Cutsinger responded. "Hurt's waiting for you."

Cooper only heard every other word the man said, but understood enough to get the gist. Patrick had invited him to the base for a meeting this morning. In the past, Cooper might've been upset with the man for continuing to want to butt into his life, but this morning, after kissing Kiera the night before and learning that she was open to going out with him, he was hard-pressed to be annoyed about anything.

He pushed open the door to his former commander's office and stopped in his tracks. He'd expected Patrick to be alone, but instead there was another man already sitting in one of the chairs in front of the large desk. Cooper didn't recognize him, but immediately knew he was either currently a Special Forces operative, or used to be. It wasn't something he could explain to someone who wasn't in their small circle. It just was.

His dark hair and brown eyes might lure some people into thinking he was a pretty boy, but they'd be wrong. Lethalness seemed to ooze from his pores even though he was simply sitting there.

Without thought, Cooper reached up to his left ear and pressed on his hearing aid. He felt it shift inside his ear canal, and he sighed in relief when he heard Hurt's chair squeal as the man stood.

"Thanks for coming, Coop," Hurt said.

Cooper concentrated on the other man's lips, and that, along with the amplification of his hearing aid, was able to help him understand him. It was a relief. He instinctively wanted to be on top of his game with the stranger.

"No problem. What's up?"

"I'd like you to meet a friend of mine. John Keegan...otherwise known as Tex."

Cooper turned to the other man and held out his hand. "*The* Tex?"

"The one and only," Tex answered with a small smile on his face as he shook his hand.

"Wow. It's really good to meet you."

Tex smiled. "Same. I've heard good things about you too and when Hurt called and asked for my help, I decided to take a trip out here. It's been a while since I've seen my friends."

Cooper knew about Tex. Hurt had talked about him quite often. A former SEAL, Tex had lost his leg, and now helped the commander—and probably a lot of other top-secret teams—with missions. He was a computer genius, and even though Cooper didn't know most of what the man did, he knew enough to know the SEALs and US government were lucky to have him on their side.

"Is everything all right?" Cooper asked Hurt. "Why's Tex here?"

"As you probably know, Tex lives on the east coast with his wife, Melody. He assists me and many other commanders around the country in gathering intel. He knows a lot of military men, retired and active duty, SEALs and Delta Force operatives who were either injured on duty or who have had enough of the teams."

Cooper eyed Tex a little more closely as Hurt continued. His initial reaction to Tex, before he knew he was the infamous former SEAL, had been correct, it was nice to know he hadn't lost all of his intuitiveness after being injured and away from the teams.

"I asked him to come down and spend a few days talking with you. I know you've met with the Navy psychologists, but there's no one who knows what you're going through better than someone who has been in your shoes."

Tex interrupted Patrick at that point. "Look, I have no idea what you're going through with your hearing. I have to deal with my leg giving me fits now and then, but it's not the same as losing my hearing, sight, or something else. I'm not here to tell you how to deal with that. Hurt asked me to talk with you about my transition to civilian life."

Cooper blinked. That so wasn't what he'd thought the other man was going to say. He'd had lots of people tell him how he should deal with the loss of his hearing and what to do with the rest of his life. But no one understood what it was like to try to transition from constantly being on call for his country and flying off at a moment's notice, to sitting around an apartment with no one needing him and no chance of *getting* that call.

His first inclination was to tell Tex to fuck off, that he was transitioning just fine, thank you very much, but then he thought about Kiera. He wanted to be worthy of her, and he was afraid if he didn't get his head screwed on straight and figure out what he wanted to do, he'd lose her. Maybe this former SEAL could help him.

"I can't say that I'm thrilled with Hurt going behind my back, but I wouldn't mind having a beer or two with you. But not at a bar. I can't hear shit."

Tex chuckled. "Not a problem."

"Now, if we're done bonding, I need to get going."

"You get a job I don't know about, Coop?" Hurt asked, leaning forward in his chair.

Cooper smirked. "No, Dad. I'm volunteering at the deaf school you guilted me into going to a few weeks ago."

The look that spread across Hurt's face could only be described as smug. "Let me guess...Ms. Hamilton's classroom?"

"Fuck off," Cooper said without heat.

"Ms. Hamilton?" Tex queried.

"She's a teacher at the school. I thought it might do Coop some good to see how easily kids can adapt to a life without being able to hear."

"And it wasn't a bonus that Kiera was friends with Julie?" Cooper asked.

"You still owe me for sending her to you," Tex told the commander.

Hurt smiled and rolled his eyes. Then he turned back to Cooper and got serious. "Kiera is a wonderful person. She works hard and is a good friend to Julie. But more than that...I like you, Coop. And if you got together with a friend of my wife's, I'd see you more. And I'd like that too."

Coop didn't know exactly what to say to that. But it felt good. Damn good to know that his former commander was more than just a boss. He was a friend too.

"Now...get the hell out of my office so I can get some work done," Hurt said, ending the touchy-feely conversation. "And say hello to Kiera for me."

Cooper and Tex both stood. They gave chin lifts to Patrick and headed out of his office.

"Hey, Coop," Cutter called out.

Cooper didn't hear him and continued toward the door. Tex touched Cooper's arm and gestured toward the administrative assistant with his head.

Fighting the urge to apologize for not hearing the summons, Cooper turned to the older man and raised his eyebrows in question.

"Wolf and the rest of his team have challenged you and Tex to a duel...so to speak. They think you guys are going soft now that you're retired. Tonight. Eighteen hundred. On the beach."

Cooper's eyes gleamed. "You wanna join us, old man?" he asked.

Cutter smiled. "Fuck yeah."

"See you later," Cooper said

"Later," Cutter responded.

As he and Tex were walking to their cars in the parking lot, the other man commented, "To be honest, I don't know why Hurt asked me down here. Don't get me wrong, I'm thrilled to be able to hang out with my friends, but you seem like you're doing just fine."

Cooper shrugged. "Maybe. Maybe not. But I'd love to hear your story. I haven't heard the story of how you met your wife."

Tex smiled. "I pretty much cyber stalked her."

Shocked, Cooper stared at the man in disbelief.

Tex chuckled. "We met online. She was being stalked and ghosted on me. I tracked her down."

"And her stalker was caught?" Cooper asked.

Tex nodded.

"I can't wait to hear this story."

"And I'll tell it to you...over a couple beers."

"I'm looking forward to it." And for once, Cooper wasn't telling someone what he thought they wanted to hear. He meant it.

The two men pounded on each other's backs and climbed into their respective cars.

As curious as Cooper was to hear Tex's story, all thoughts of the other man and the upcoming competition on the beach fled. He was looking more forward to seeing Kiera again.

## CHAPTER 4

KIERA SMILED as Cooper knocked on the door to her classroom. She'd been informed by the principal that Cooper requested to volunteer with her class today. Even though he'd been at the school many times over the last couple months, he hadn't ever been in her room. She'd tried not to be hurt by that, but couldn't deny it had.

She'd just gotten her first graders settled down with their tablets when Cooper arrived. The students were watching videos of a book being read and signed at the same time. Getting the youngsters familiar with both the written word, a picture, and the sign for the word was imperative in their cognitive development. They typically learned slower than children who could hear, but she'd found that most were starved for knowledge and, once they got the hang of reading, were extremely quick to pick it up and correlate words with the correct signs.

She walked over to greet him and blushed as he stared at her lips as if he wanted to devour her right there in the doorway. "Hey."

"Hey. Is this a bad time?"

Kiera shook her head. "Not at all. I just got them settled with books. How come you haven't ever volunteered in my classroom before?"

"I'm not great with kids this young," Cooper admitted as he followed her into the room. "The older ones I can impress with my background, but little ones aren't as easily swayed."

"You'll be fine," Kiera told him, his insecurity somehow making him all the more appealing to her. "Wait here while I get their attention," she told Cooper, pointing to a spot at the front. When he nodded, she walked around the room, putting her hand on each child's shoulder and signing something to them.

When she had everyone's attention, she signed at the same time as she spoke. "Class, this is Cooper Nelson. He is here to read with you."

A little girl threw up her hand in question.

"Yes, Becca?"

The little girl's hands moved slowly, but she was obviously asking a question about Cooper as she gestured to him several times.

Kiera repeated her question for all the other children in the class. She found that sometimes the children had a hard time reading someone else's signs and it was good practice for everyone to see the same signs done several times.

"Becca asked if Mr. Nelson knows sign language. She also asked if he was deaf. He knows some sign language, but he just started learning, like all of you. Cooper can hear a little out of his left ear, but wears a hearing aid like some of you do. He is completely deaf in his right ear."

A little boy's hand went up, and Kiera pointed at him and said while signing, "Yes, Billy?"

Billy's hands moved as he asked his question.

Cooper put his hand on Kiera's arm and asked, "Can I answer?"

She smiled up at him and nodded.

Cooper kneeled on the ground and turned his head to the kids and pointed to his hearing aid. Then he signed, slowly, and imprecisely, "I was standing too close to a..." He paused and looked up at Kiera and shrugged.

Her heart melted. He was trying so hard, and getting on the same level as the kids was something a lot of people didn't realize made a huge difference. She quickly said and signed "explosion." He smiled at her and turned back to the children, who had been watching the two adults with wide eyes.

"Explosion," Cooper signed. "It made me lose my hearing."

Six children immediately raised their hands with questions. Kiera chuckled.

They spent the next twenty minutes playing question and answer. Cooper painstakingly tried to answer each question and Kiera helped him with the correct sign when he didn't know it, which was often.

Cooper answered questions about whether he had any scars, if he was married, if he had children, how old he was, what he did for a living and if the explosion had hurt. He'd answered them as honestly as he could and didn't laugh at some of the silly questions the kids asked.

The awe and adoration was clear to see on most of the children's faces. It wasn't often they'd seen a man like Cooper—a strong, tall, *masculine* man—make the effort to talk to them in their language. His obvious lack of expertise made him seem more approachable to them, as did his constant laughing at his ineptitude.

Just when Kiera was about to tell the children to get back to work, a little boy sitting in the back of the classroom slowly raised his hand. She hid her surprise. Frankie was small for his age and wasn't making much progress. He was very reluctant to sign and hadn't made any friends in the class since he'd been there. He frequently resorted to pushing the kids in his class when he couldn't understand them or when he wanted his way.

Kiera knew his attitude was a result of his tumultuous home life and starting in a new school and her heart hurt for him. Frankie's father was excited about the chance for his son to be in the special school. They'd moved down to Riverton from Los Angeles for a fresh start after a contentious divorce. His ex-wife was a drug addict who was deemed unfit to have custody of their son. Until recently, she'd been allowed to have supervised visitations with Frankie, but after slipping away from the court-ordered supervisor and taking Frankie to the mall to a drug drop, she'd had all parental rights stripped from her.

Kiera understood that the little boy was probably having issues dealing with all the upheaval in his life, but it had been two months since he'd started school and he wasn't getting any better. The fact that he'd engaged enough to raise his hand and ask a question was almost a miracle at this point.

She pointed at the skinny boy and signed, "Yes, Frankie?"

He mostly used the alphabet to spell out his question, but it was understandable, if not painful to wait for him to get through.

Kiera swallowed and flicked her eyes to Cooper before repeating the question for the rest of the class. "Frankie asked what his tough military friends thought of Cooper using his hands to speak in such a sissy way."

A few of the kids gasped and whipped their heads around to gaze at Frankie with wide eyes. Kiera hadn't realized that was what Frankie thought of sign language. It was as heartbreaking as it was shocking.

Bless Cooper, he didn't even blink at the question. He got up and went over to where Frankie was sitting. When he got there, he sat on his butt and awkwardly crossed his legs. Then he proceeded to blow Kiera's mind.

He used mostly finger spelling, as Frankie had, and not once did he look to Kiera for a sign. "My friends are jealous that I have my own secret language. Believe it or not, Frankie, my team had our own hand signals for stuff. This," he made a movement with his hands that Kiera didn't recognize, "meant danger. And this," he did it again, making another sign that clearly wasn't American Sign Language, "meant bad guy ahead. I don't know who told you that sign language was sissy, but it absolutely isn't. It's cool. The coolest thing I've ever tried to learn. I can talk to you, your classmates, or Ms. Hamilton, and people who aren't deaf can't understand me. It's like being an undercover spy right under people's noses. I love knowing a secret language, even if I'm not very good at it yet."

If Kiera hadn't been watching Frankie carefully, she would've missed it, but his eyes got big and she could literally see the knowledge that a big, strong man like Cooper thought sign language was cool sinking into his psyche.

She'd tried for months to get Frankie to show an ounce of interest in anything she did or said, to no avail. But with one painstakingly finger-spelled answer, Cooper had somehow bonded with the young boy in a way she'd rarely seen before.

Swallowing hard so she wouldn't burst into tears, Kiera waved her hand in the air to get the children's attention. She sighed, "Now that we have all met Cooper, time to get back to your lessons."

The kids all nodded and shuffled back to various places around the room with their tablets. There were beanbags strewn around the classroom, as well as small couches, and big fluffy rugs... more than enough choices for the children to settle in comfortably somewhere.

She looked over at Frankie and Cooper and caught the tail end of Cooper's question to the little boy. "...me sit with you while you read?"

Frankie nodded his head and Kiera watched in awe as Cooper and her troublemaker student shifted so they were sitting facing each other, knees touching, with the tablet off to their right. Frankie reached out and turned it on, activating the story he'd been reading before the interruption.

Over the next thirty minutes, Kiera watched from the corner of her eye as Frankie and Cooper went through one story, then another, then finally a third. She'd never seen the little boy as interested and engrossed in a lesson as he was during that half hour. He and Cooper signed each word as the narrator of the book instructed. They smiled at each other often and at one point, Frankie even reached out and corrected one of Cooper's signs.

It was time for lunch and Kiera corralled the children and got them lined up to head down to the lunchroom. There were several monitors who assisted the kids who needed it in getting their lunch trays and generally kept order in the large cafeteria. As they were waiting for a monitor to lead everyone down the hall, Kiera eavesdropped on the conversation between Frankie and Cooper.

"Will you come back?" Frankie finger spelled.

"Yes," Cooper signed.

"When?"

Cooper paused for a long moment then finally signed, "If you want me to, I'll be here every day."

Kiera gasped. He couldn't tell Frankie that. It would crush the little boy when he didn't actually show up every day. Before she could rush over and do damage control, Frankie surprised her.

"Don't say it if you don't mean it," the little boy spelled out.

Cooper placed one of his large hands on Frankie's thin shoulder and spelled out with his other hand. "I don't say things I don't mean. Do you want to learn a secret sign me and my military friends use?" Cooper asked in a mixture of letters and signs.

Frankie eagerly signed, "Yes."

"Okay, but it's super-secret and it's a man code. You can only greet other men this way. Okay?"

Frankie impatiently signed once again. "Yes."

"Watch carefully," Cooper signed, then lifted his chin in the way Kiera had seen him greet his friends in the past.

She used her hand to cover the smile on her face.

Frankie furrowed his little brow and tried to imitate Cooper.

"Pretty good, but instead of making it look like a nod, just lift your chin a little bit instead." Cooper demonstrated again.

Frankie mirrored him and this time, amazingly, he did it. The chin lift he gave Cooper was a mini-version of the badass "hey" Cooper gave his friends.

"That's it! You did it. Good job. Now remember… only manly men get that chin lift. It's our secret hello and goodbye code." He glanced over at Kiera and winked, then turned back to Frankie. "I'll see you tomorrow Frankie, right?"

Frankie nodded and had a big smile on his face. The first time Kiera could remember the little boy ever doing so since he'd started school.

The line started to move, and Cooper stood up straight and looked down at Frankie. He gave him the chin lift and signed, "Goodbye."

Frankie returned the chin lift and sign, then walked proudly out of the room behind his classmates.

Kiera shut the door behind her students and walked directly to Cooper.

"I—"

She didn't let him get any other words out before standing on her tiptoes and putting both hands on either side of his face. She tugged his head toward hers and planted her lips on his. His arms immediately locked around her and he pulled her into him so they were touching from hips to chest.

He let her control the kiss for a moment, then took over. Devouring her mouth as if he hadn't seen her in years instead of the night before. They finally broke apart, but Cooper didn't let go of her. He kept her plastered to the front of his body as he asked, "What was that for?"

"You are a miracle worker," Kiera told him.

He chuckled. "Don't think Mother Theresa would agree with you on that one, sweetheart."

Kiera shook her head. "Seriously. I've been trying to get Frankie to respond to me with a tenth of the enthusiasm he showed you today...with no luck. And you spent thirty minutes with him and he's like a completely different child."

"All he needed was some attention," Cooper protested. "I didn't do anything special."

"No, that's not it," Kiera insisted.

"I know." Cooper's voice had dropped until it was barely audible, but Kiera didn't interrupt him. "Someone's been filling his head with shit about how a real man acts. I think seeing me, a former Special Forces operative using sign language, legitimized it somehow. All I had to do was show him that it's okay to talk with my hands. That it doesn't make him any less of a boy. I want ten minutes in a room with whoever has been filling his head with that shit. Probably his dad."

"It's not him," Kiera told him, running her fingernails lightly down the back of Cooper's neck where she'd rested her hands. "His dad loves him to pieces. He's a single dad who is working his ass off to get his son what he needs to succeed."

"Whoever it is should be shot," Cooper murmured, then lowered his head to the space between Kiera's neck and shoulder. He inhaled and nuzzled the skin there.

Kiera felt goosebumps move over her at the feel

of his lips against her bare skin. She tugged lightly on his hair and he lifted his head to look at her.

"Are you really going to come every day like you told Frankie? You can't lie to these kids, Cooper. If you tell them something, you have to follow through."

"I wasn't lying. I really would like to stop by every day...if that's all right," he finished uncertainly.

"It's all right," Kiera reassured him immediately. "But I'm afraid you'll get bored."

"Kiera, I spent almost eight years of my life getting shot at, blowing shit up, and putting my life on the line for my country. Spending time with kids, helping them learn, helping myself learn, sounds like heaven."

Kiera swallowed hard. She didn't know any men, not one, who would say something like Cooper just had. "Okay."

"Okay." Cooper smiled at her, then pulled her hips harder into his own. She could feel his erection against her core and her inner muscles clenched. God. "You want to have dinner tonight?"

"Yes," she answered immediately. She wanted as much of Cooper's time as he'd give her. It didn't matter that it was a school night. It didn't matter that she wasn't playing hard to get. If Cooper wanted to spend time with her, she would grab on to that with both hands.

He smiled down at her. "I have to do a thing with the SEALs on the beach at six, but maybe I can pick you up afterwards?"

"What thing?"

Cooper rolled his eyes. "Me and two other retired SEALs were challenged by an active-duty team."

"Challenged how?" Kiera asked, tilting her head.

"Not to the death, if that's what you're thinking," Cooper grinned. "You should've seen your face. Just to a friendly physical competition on the beach. Sit-ups, running with the Zodiac, swimming, that sort of thing."

"Can I come watch?"

She saw some sort of emotion move through Cooper's eyes, but couldn't interpret it. She hurried to say, "If it's not allowed, that's okay, I just thought it might be fun to watch you in action."

"You'd like that?" he questioned.

"Seeing you and a bunch of other SEALs, hope-fully in nothing but short shorts, running around on the beach flexing and trying to prove who's stronger and more badass? Hell yeah, I'd like that," Kiera told him with a smile.

His hands moved to her waist and he started to tickle her. Kiera screeched and tried to wiggle out of his grasp. "Cooper, stop! I'm extremely ticklish!" She couldn't stop giggling, and her hands pushing at his chest were ineffective to stop the intimate torture.

"You want to look at other men's bodies, Kiera?"

She giggled some more and said, "No, just yours!"

"But you said you wanted to check out my friends' asses."

"No, I didn't. I'll only look at your ass…swear!"

"Promise?"

Kiera couldn't stop giggling. Coopers fingers might've been tickling her, but she loved having his hands on her…and his playfulness. "I promise…please…"

"Please what?" Cooper asked, putting his arms back around her and yanking her into his rock-hard body once more.

Kiera looked up at him then and brought her arms up between them, signing as she said, "Please kiss me."

Cooper glanced at the door, and while Kiera appreciated his awareness of where they were and the fact anyone could come inside the classroom at any time, at the moment, she didn't care. She needed his lips on hers again.

Without a word, Cooper did as she asked. He kissed her as if his life depended on it. Slow and fast, deep and shallow. It wasn't just a kiss, he learned what she liked, that she moaned deep in her throat when he sucked on her tongue and dug her nails into his chest when he nibbled on her bottom lip.

Five minutes later, Cooper pulled back and looked down at her. He placed a hand on her forehead and ran it gently over her blonde hair, smoothing it down as he went. "Do you really want to come tonight?"

Kiera nodded.

"I'll pick you up at five-twenty?"

She nodded again.

"Means a lot to me, Kiera."

"What does?"

"That you want to be involved in my world. Not just be with me because I have a good body, or because I'm good with the kids in your class."

"Cooper, I wouldn't care if you were a world-class chess player...I'd want to be there to support you because you enjoy doing it. And while I won't deny that I can't wait to see your body tonight, that's not why I'm with you."

"Why *are* you?" he asked.

Kiera could see the insecurity in the badass man

in front of her and it made him that much more real to her. "I've never been as attracted to anyone as I am to you. You're a good person. From the first time you walked into the school, I could tell that you were uncomfortable, but you didn't let it stop you from jumping in with both feet. You aren't afraid to admit that you don't understand something, and so far, you haven't been discouraged when learning a new language gets tough. You see me—not just the teacher, not just Julie's friend, but me. I'm not afraid to be myself around you, and even though I'm scared to death you're gonna take one look at my naked body and ask yourself what the hell you're doing with an almost-forty-year-old woman...I can't wait to make love with you."

"Damn," Cooper breathed.

"You asked," Kiera said with a smile.

"That I did. And for the record, the feeling is definitely mutual. You don't see only the SEAL when you look at me, at least I don't think you do. You see me. So I get what you're saying. And no worries, Kiera..." Cooper moved his hands until they were grasping the globes of her ass and pulled her into him until she was standing on her tiptoes. Their crotches were aligned, and Kiera could feel every inch of his hard cock against her. She shifted in his grasp and tried to get closer...to no avail.

"I'm going to love every inch of your body. Have no doubt." He leaned down and took her mouth in one more hard, intimate kiss before pulling back and putting a couple inches of space between their bodies.

"Wear comfortable clothes tonight. Jeans, blouse, flip-flops...after we kick the SEALs' asses, I'll shower and we'll go somewhere casual for dinner. Burgers all right?"

"Absolutely."

As if he couldn't help himself, Cooper leaned down and kissed Kiera once more then stepped away from her and dropped his hands. "See you tonight then."

Kiera nodded, then gave him a chin lift.

His lips quirked, and he said, "Sorry hon, that's reserved for us men." Then he winked and was gone.

Kiera sat at her desk to eat lunch and thought about Cooper. She'd known the man a few weeks now, ever since he'd begun volunteering at the school, but somehow over the last twenty-four hours he'd become not just a man she'd like to get to know better, but one she didn't think she could live without.

Smiling big, she finished her lunch and thought about what she was going to wear that night. Yeah, seeing Cooper and his friends rolling around the sand in minimal clothing certainly wasn't a hardship. Not at all.

# CHAPTER 5

Kɪᴇʀᴀ sᴀᴛ on a sand dune that overlooked a section of beach on Coronado Island. Cooper had picked her up right at five-twenty...but they'd still been ten minutes late to the beach. He'd taken one look at her in her skinny jeans, flip-flops, navy blue scoop-neck shirt that had a picture of a military man aiming a rifle and lying in a puddle of water with the words, *Stay Low, Go Fast. Kill First, Die Last. One Shot, One Kill. No Luck, All Skill*, and her blonde hair flowing freely around her shoulders instead of confined back in the bun she usually wore at the school, and he'd backed her against the front door and proceeded to ravish her.

It had taken his phone vibrating in his pocket with a text from a man named Cutter, warning him not to be late, to break them apart. He'd closed his eyes, rested his forehead against hers and said in a low, controlled voice, "You're gonna be the death of me."

Kiera had simply responded, "But what a way to go."

Now she was sitting on a giant pile of sand with four other women, watching as their men competed against each other down near the surf.

"I'll never get tired of this," Julie stated with a sigh.

One of the other women—she'd been introduced as Caroline—agreed. "Right? When Wolf told me he'd challenged Tex and two other former SEALs to a physical battle, there was no way I wasn't going to be here."

"I'm just thankful Fiona could watch our kids on such short notice," a Navy wife named Jessyka said.

"Anyone bring any popcorn?" the last woman in their group, who had been introduced as Cheyenne, asked.

Kiera had liked the other women immediately. They'd made her feel comfortable and not at all awkward, as she usually did when she met new people. Julie had mentioned all three of them at one point in past conversations, but this was the first time she was getting to spend any time with them.

"You know what...Tex is hot," Cheyenne observed.

Jessyka rolled her eyes. "You do remember that you're a married woman, right?" she asked her friend.

"Of course. Faulkner won't let me forget it, not that I would want to. But there's nothing wrong with looking. And I don't think I've ever seen so much of Tex before."

Kiera agreed wholeheartedly. She knew the other SEALs knew Cooper's new friend Tex, but wasn't exactly sure how he was connected to everyone. She let it go. The spectacle below them was definitely too drool-worthy to think about anything else at the moment. The men had stripped off their T-shirts and were currently wrestling with each other...she wasn't sure exactly what they were doing, but didn't really care either.

"I swear to God, every time I see Cutter, I send up a prayer that Benny will look just like him in a decade or so," Jessyka murmured, resting her chin on her hand as she gazed down at the men. "He's just so...manly looking."

"Manly looking?" Julie laughed. "As if the other guys aren't?"

"You know what I mean. He looks distinguished. His graying hair and beard, his broad shoulders… even the hint of gray in his chest hair is fucking hot."

"Is he dating anyone?" Julie asked. "Patrick tells me all about how awesome he's been since he's started working as his admin assistant, but he doesn't tell me about anyone's love life."

Caroline shrugged. "I don't think so, but Wolf is the same way. They'll gossip like girls with each other and in the office, but then he'll tell me that it's a man code thing and he can't share details. Sometimes I wish our men weren't so honorable."

Everyone chuckled but Kiera inhaled sharply when a foot came shooting toward Cooper's face.

"Relax," Cheyenne soothed, resting her hand on Kiera's arm. "Your man has this."

And he did. As soon as the foot moved toward him, Cooper had grabbed hold and wrenched it upward, throwing one of the SEALs to the sand on his back. The men all laughed and continued to try to beat the crap out of each other. At least that's what it looked like to her.

"Can anyone tell who's winning?" Cheyenne asked.

"Does it matter?" Jessyka asked.

Cheyenne laughed. "I guess not. I know that I'll reap the benefits of all that bottled-up testosterone tonight though."

Kiera giggled along with the other women and shifted in her seat. She'd love to be on the receiving end of Cooper's bottled-up hormones. The thought excited her. She liked the thought of her man being romantic as much as the next woman, but the image of Cooper ravishing her and taking what he wanted, how he wanted, and as hard as he wanted, was a huge turn-on.

They continued to watch as the men put each other through their paces. Like Cheyenne, Kiera couldn't tell who was winning and what exactly each competition was, but watching the men move was like seeing poetry in motion. They were all built, buff, and in extremely good shape. It was obvious the three retired SEALs had no problem keeping up with the active-duty guys. Even Tex, with his prosthetic leg, made the physical exertion look easy.

After about an hour, and a final dip in the ocean to rinse off the sand, the men all shook each other's hands. Five men headed up the sand dune toward their women, while the rest gave each other chin lifts and headed for the parking lot or the offices.

Kiera's lips twitched at seeing the chin lifts back and forth, it reminded her of little Frankie and how awesome Cooper had been with him. She met his eyes as he climbed the slight rise to get to them.

He came right up to her and took her head in his hands and kissed her. It didn't even seem awkward to have him stake his claim so publicly and carnally.

"Hey," she said when he finally pulled back.

Cooper shook his head and pointed to his ear, indicating he wasn't wearing his hearing aid.

Kiera hadn't seen him remove it, but it made sense. It probably wouldn't have been good to get sand under it, not to mention the sea water. Not knowing how he felt about signing in front of his friends, she hesitated. But she shouldn't have. As if he could read her mind, he half-signed, half-spelled, "You think I'd say all that stuff to Frankie then be embarrassed to sign in front of my friends?"

Kiera smiled back and quickly signed, "No, but I didn't want to do anything that might jeopardize my chance of getting some at a later date."

Cooper barked out a laugh and grinned from ear to ear.

"No fair, man," Wolf complained. "Want to let us in on the joke?"

Kiera looked to Cooper, who was still watching

Wolf. She quickly signed, "Wolf wants to know what's funny."

"Nothing you need to know about," Cooper said out loud to his friend, still grinning. "You know, I never really thought twice about the nonverbal signals we always used on the teams, but it's amazing how similar some are to ASL, American Sign Language."

Kiera loved that he had no problem speaking with his friends, even without his hearing aid and without being able to hear their responses.

She barely heard the other men agreeing and mumbling about needing showers. She only had eyes for Cooper. Every moment she spent around him had her falling harder. All the weeks she'd gotten to know him during his time spent at the school had morphed her feelings from respect and admiration, to lust and longing. She couldn't say she loved him yet, but she knew it wouldn't take long. Not if he continued blowing her away with his awesomeness.

"I need a shower," he signed.

"Yes, you do," she returned.

His lips quirked. "Don't be shy. Tell me what you think."

"I will. Hope that isn't a problem."

"No. I love it. Come on. Let me shower, put my ear back in, and we'll go."

She loved how he'd phrased that…put my ear back in. It was casual and not at all self-conscious. It was perfect.

"How long have you known Cooper?" Cheyenne asked as the group headed down off the sand dune toward the offices and showers.

"About two months, I think," Kiera told her. She turned to Cooper and had a quick conversation with him, confirming the date before turning back to Cheyenne. "Yup, two months."

"It really is cool how you can talk to him like that," Julie said quietly.

Kiera shrugged. "ASL is a language. Just like Spanish, German, or any other. I think others view deaf people as handicapped, when in reality they're just bilingual."

"That's so true," Jessyka said, the awe clear in her tone. "I never really thought of it that way before."

"I'm going to see if I can start a training program to teach the SEALs under my command sign language. I know most of the guys have some sort of pigeon non verbal signs they already use, but I think it could be beneficial if everyone knew the same signals and language," Patrick informed the group.

"I'm in," Wolf said immediately.

"Me too," the large man next to Cheyenne agreed.

"I know all the guys on our team would be up for it," Jessyka's husband agreed.

"It might be a while, don't get too excited," the commander warned. "I need to find an acceptable teacher. It's not like I can bring in any ol' teacher off the street...no offense intended, Kiera."

She waved off his concern. "No, I get it. The things you guys do are top secret, and even though it's just words, you want to get someone who understands what it is you do and the situations you get into, so you can learn the most appropriate words. There's no need to necessarily learn things like apple or asparagus."

Cooper tapped her on the shoulder and signed, "What's he saying?"

Quickly, Kiera brought him up to speed on the conversation. Cooper didn't respond, but he got an introspective look on his face. She brought her hands up to ask him what he was thinking, but was interrupted by Cheyenne's screech.

"Faulkner! Put me down!"

Her husband had slung her over his shoulder and was striding toward the parking lot.

"See you tomorrow, Dude!" Wolf called out, chuckling.

Kiera could hear Cheyenne's giggles as she half-heartedly tried to wiggle out of her husband's grasp. She couldn't hear whatever it was the SEAL said to his wife, but it made Cheyenne go limp, and he swung her around until he was cradling her in his arms as he kept walking.

Kiera saw Cheyenne put one hand on his face and smile up at him before they got too far away to see specifics anymore. She remembered the other woman's comment about benefiting from her husband's testosterone and got turned on all over again.

They arrived at the door to the offices and Kiera felt a hand on her face and turned to Cooper. "Give me twenty minutes to shower?" he asked softly.

She nodded, and he kissed her briefly on the lips then disappeared into the offices with the rest of the men.

"I'm gonna head out and get the kids and meet Kason at home," Jessyka told them. "It was good to meet you, Kiera. Hopefully we'll see more of you around."

"Same. See ya," Kiera answered.

She sank onto a bench next to Julie to wait for Cooper.

"So...you and Coop? Officially?" Julie asked with a smile.

Kiera merely smiled. "Yup."

"Awesome," her friend breathed, nudging her with her shoulder.

"I have to say, he looks like he's doing really well," Caroline observed. "I mean, we're not best friends or anything, but Wolf told me he was having a hard time after he was injured. He didn't want to be around anyone and never went anywhere without his hearing aid. I'm so glad to see him relaxing a bit."

Kiera nodded. "Yeah, I've noticed the same change. When he first started volunteering at my school, he didn't say much to anyone and kinda kept to himself a lot. But the more he helped the kids, the more he seemed to realize that being deaf wasn't the end of the world."

"I saw you drag him out of my party," Julie noted. "You think that has anything to do with his new and improved attitude?"

"No. I have nothing to do with it," Kiera protested.

"I think you're wrong," Julie countered. "I'm not saying you're wrong that the kids and volunteering have helped him. Patrick wouldn't have highly suggested he do it if he didn't think it would help. But these guys...they're a lot more sensitive than they'd have the world believe. They get shot, no problem, they can suck it up and deal, looking forward to getting back on the front lines. But being injured enough that they can't do what they've spent the better part of their adult lives perfecting? It hits them harder than nonmilitary guys. Especially if they're single. They start thinking they aren't good enough. That no one will ever love them the way they are. The feelings escalate until they think all anyone can see is that disability. A scar. A limp. Their loss of hearing."

The women were silent for a long moment, then Julie went on after laughing nervously. "I'm not an expert, but I've been reading up on this and watching Patrick's men. I'm telling you, I can see a difference between the Cooper of a week ago and the man who was messing around with his friends on the beach tonight. I think you're one reason why he's suddenly come to grips with his loss of hearing, Kiera."

She knew she was blushing, but Kiera managed a shrug. "I'm not looking to be his hero."

"But apparently you are anyway," Caroline stated

evenly. Then smiled. "Welcome to the weird and wacky world of loving a Navy SEAL. Retired or not, your man is every inch a SEAL."

Kiera smiled. "Do I get a pin or something for joining the club?"

"A pin for what?" Cooper asked as he strode out the door.

Kiera popped up from her seat and turned to him. He looked good. Really good. His hair was still damp from his shower and she could smell the soap on his skin. She shook her head. "Nothing. Girl talk."

"Sweet Jesus, I'm in trouble," he teased. "Girl talk with Caroline and Julie can't mean anything good."

"Shut it, buddy," Julie said as she stood.

"Be afraid, be very afraid," Caroline deadpanned.

Their men came out the door then and Wolf asked, "Afraid of what?"

Kiera shook her head. She couldn't help it. The guys were funny.

"Never mind. Ready to go?" Caroline asked her husband.

"If you are," Wolf responded.

"Babe, do you mind if we stop at the hospital on the way home? I'd like to visit a sailor who just arrived," Patrick asked after kissing Julie on the temple tenderly.

"Of course not," Julie said. "A SEAL?"

"Nope. Just a regular sailor. He apparently got really sick on the aircraft carrier he was on and had his appendix taken out onboard, but there were complications and they ended up flying him home. He could use some cheering up, as his family hasn't arrived yet."

"What are we waiting for?" Julie asked, pulling on Patrick's hand. "Let's go. See you later, Kiera!" she called out as she towed her husband toward the parking lot.

"Alone at last," Cooper said after the other two couples were out of sight.

"Got your ear back in?" Kiera asked.

Cooper nodded. "Yup. Although I'm not sure I'm up for a crowded restaurant. How do you feel about takeout?"

"Love it," Kiera agreed. "I'd much rather hang out with you in the peace and quiet of one of our apartments than yell over a nasty, germy table anyway."

Cooper laughed. "Me too. And I hadn't thought of restaurant tables as nasty and germy until now, thank you very much."

"Oh, believe me, they are. Most of the time no one even wipes them down between customers. They're petri dishes of nastiness just waiting for a victim to latch onto and cause havoc in their digestive system."

He leaned over and kissed the top of Kiera's head. "I love the way you think."

She looked up at him in confusion. "You love that I think about how germy and disgusting tables in restaurants are?"

"No. I love that I have no idea what's going to come out of your mouth. I love knowing that when I'm around you, I'm gonna laugh at some point during our time together. I love that you say what you're thinking. I love watching you sign with your students and that you can make them smile as easily as you do me."

Kiera stared up at Cooper, not sure how to respond. He might be ten years younger than her, but he was more mature than every man she'd dated. He never blew smoke up her ass and every word out of his mouth was sincere and made her fall for him even more.

"Come on," he said, obviously seeing how flustered she was. "Let's go find something to eat and then relax. I didn't really mean to start out our first date by ignoring you in favor of showing up my SEAL brethren."

"But I got to see you almost naked," Kiera blurted. "I'd say it was a good start."

Cooper barked out a laugh then ran his hand over her hair, smoothing it away from her face tenderly. "See? You're funny. Come on. I'm starved."

Kiera melted into Cooper's side when, instead of taking her hand, he put his arm around her shoulders and pulled her into him. She snaked her arm around his waist and they walked toward the parking lot together.

# CHAPTER 6

HOURS LATER, Cooper sat on Kiera's tan suede couch, relaxed and content. Kiera was leaning against the armrest, her legs resting over his lap, and had been sipping wine since they'd finished dinner.

*The Green Mile* was playing on the television, with subtitles of course, but neither of them were watching it. They'd started out the night on opposite sides of the sofa, but when she'd complained that her feet hurt, he'd offered to give her a foot massage and now, here they were.

Halfway through dinner, he'd asked if she wouldn't mind signing as she spoke with him, to give him practice. She'd agreed and they'd been talking nonstop since.

"What was it like growing up with a deaf parent?" Cooper asked.

Kiera shrugged. "Like any other kid, I expect. Since I don't have anything to compare it to, I couldn't really say."

"Were you teased?"

"Not really," Kiera said, then picked up her wine glass, took a sip, and placed it back on the table next to the couch so she could continue signing as she spoke. "When I was at school, I didn't sign. When I was at home, I signed and spoke, just like I'm doing now." She shrugged. "I never really thought much of it. Signing comes as naturally to me as someone who grew up speaking, say, Spanish in the home and English outside of it."

"I think you're amazing," Cooper told her, squeezing her leg. "I find it incredibly difficult to coordinate my hands with what I'm hearing and making it all work together."

"Give yourself a break, Cooper. You haven't been doing this very long. It takes practice. Just like being a SEAL does. You didn't learn how to do some of the stuff you did overnight."

He nodded. "You're right, I know you are. But I've never been a patient man."

The look of desire in her eyes made him swallow

hard. As did her subtle shifting in her seat. He wanted her. Now. He wanted her naked and on her knees in front of him, sucking him off. Wanted her laid out on her couch, wet and ready for him. Hell, he wanted her any way he could get her. Up against a wall, over her kitchen table, in the shower, in her bed. The visions he had of them making love slammed into his brain and he immediately got hard. Kiera didn't miss it.

She shifted her legs until one brushed against his erection and they both inhaled sharply. Showing her maturity, which Cooper found refreshing as hell, she said, "Patience is overrated."

He grinned and shifted until he was crouched over her. At his movements, she'd lain back. Her hands gripped his biceps and she smiled up at him. "You're beautiful," he breathed as he gazed down at her.

Her nipples were hard little peaks under her T-shirt, he could feel the heat of her body against his inner thighs as he straddled her, and her blue eyes sparkled with interest.

When she didn't respond, he said what was on his mind. "I don't want to rush this. I think it's obvious that I want you." Cooper let his body weight rest on hers for a moment, letting her feel how hard he was, how turned on, before he flexed his muscles and crouched over her again.

Her hips pressed upward, trying to follow him, but she relaxed when it was obvious he wasn't going to give her the pressure she wanted.

"Cooper," she complained, but he didn't give her a chance to beg him. He couldn't. If she did, he'd probably give in.

"I've wanted you for two months, and I'm not going to jump you in the first twenty-four hours I find out my interest is returned. I was a Navy SEAL. I've got more fortitude than that."

"You have to know I want you back," Kiera said breathlessly, staring up at him as if he was the best thing since sliced bread.

"I hoped you did, but thank you for confirming, sweetheart. But I still don't want to rush this. I want to enjoy the experience."

"What experience?"

"Making you mine. I don't want to fall into any stereotypes you might have in your mind about how a younger man operates when he's entering a relationship. Yes, I want you. I want you every way I can get you. I can't *wait* to have you, but sex isn't why I want to be with you. I admire you more than I can say. The way you work with the kids in your class.

The way you care, truly care about them. You might not want children, but I can see how much you love them. I want to get to know everything about you before I learn how your body trembles in the throes of an orgasm. I want to know what you're like in the morning before I learn how you taste after you come. I want to figure out what makes you happy and what makes you grumpy before I experience your hot, wet body squeezing my dick as you explode under me. The bottom line, sweetheart, is that as much as I want to shove your jeans down your legs and bury my face in your crotch, I want to get to know you as a woman first. Can I tell you a secret?"

Kiera swallowed hard before licking her lips and saying softly, "If it's going to blow my mind more than what you just said, I'm not sure I can handle it."

Cooper leaned down and kissed her forehead before straightening. "You can. I'm coming to realize you can handle just about anything. From the first day we met, I realized that you were my reward."

"What? I don't understand."

"I've lived my life from one day to the next. Not really thinking about the future, figuring I had my entire life to worry about that. Then after I was injured, I was struggling. I didn't want to leave my apartment, didn't want to interact with anyone because I was embarrassed that I had to ask them to repeat what they'd said to me so many times. I was bitter that I'd given so much to my country and didn't have much to show for it. Then I met you and I understood. You are my reward. My reward for all that I did. All that I sacrificed. You are the cosmos' gift to me for surviving that blast."

"Oh my God," Kiera whispered, shaking her head. "Cooper, no, that's not—"

"I didn't tell you that to freak you out."

"Major fail," she said dryly, blinking furiously to try to hold back the tears he could see pooling in her eyes.

"You're everything I ever wanted in a woman. Self-assured. Successful. Intelligent. You don't *need* me, but I'm hoping you *want* me."

"I do," she said immediately.

"All I'm saying is that from the first day I met you, I wanted you. And every day I've been near you since has only solidified that fact. Yes, I want to make love with you. I also want to fuck you. But I want to date you first. Get to know you. Have you get to know me. Is that all right?"

"Yes," Kiera answered immediately. "God, yes." She shifted under him. "But does that mean we can't...make out every now and then while we're getting to know each other?"

He chuckled. "No. We can make out. But don't think you can make me forget that I want to wait to..." He sat up on his knees, made a circle with one hand and, using the pointer finger on his other, pantomimed the crude and rude version of making love.

Kiera laughed and reached up to grab his hands. "What you just did is kinda the sign for anal sex."

Cooper immediately dropped his hands. Good Lord, the last thing he wanted to do was tell Kiera he wanted to fuck her in the ass on their first date.

But instead of being offended, she laughed at him. "If you could only see your face right now, Cooper. There are lots of dirty words I can teach you, but only if you promise not to show them to Frankie or anyone else."

Cooper knew his eyebrows had shot up in horror. "As if I would! He's seven!"

"I was only kidding. I know you wouldn't." She wrinkled her nose, which he thought was adorable, then said, "Okay then. I'll show you how to say 'fuck.' Make a peace sign with both hands." She demonstrated, holding up her hands.

Cooper mimicked her and waited with a grin on

his face. If someone had told him right after he was injured that he'd be here, kneeling over the woman he longed to make his own, learning how to say fuck in sign language, he would've kicked their ass and told them to stop messing with his mind.

"Then turn one hand so the back is facing the floor, and with the back of your other hand facing the ceiling, knock them together…it kinda looks like two bunnies going at it."

Again, she demonstrated, and Cooper could feel the dumb smile on his face. He copied her movements and she nodded up at him. "That's it."

Without a word, Cooper leaned down and kissed her. Using nothing more than his lips, he tried to show her how much she already meant to him.

Kiera tried to pull him down so he was lying on her, but he stubbornly refused to budge. Finally, realizing he wasn't going to do what she wanted, she ran her fingernails lightly up and down his biceps and gave herself over to his kiss, letting him take control.

Cooper closed his eyes and concentrated on memorizing the taste and feel of Kiera's mouth under his. How a kiss could turn him on almost to the point he thought he'd come in his pants, he didn't know, but he'd never been happier in his life.

Pulling back, he gazed down at her and waited for her eyes to open. When they did, he said softly, "It's late. I need to go."

Pouting, Kiera asked, "So soon?"

"I've been here for hours," Cooper told her.

"So soon?" Kiera repeated with a small smile.

He sat up and pulled her upright next to him. "Thank you for a wonderful first date, sweetheart. Want to grab lunch tomorrow?"

"Yes."

Her answer was immediate and heartfelt. Even though he'd had a pretty good idea she was going to agree, he was still relieved. He'd dated enough to know that many times women played games, like thinking there needed to be three days between dates, or that agreeing to see a man too soon after a first date meant he would get bored and think she wasn't worth the chase. Where they got those ideas, he'd never know.

"I'll call you and we can figure it out. Okay?"

"Sounds good. Cooper?"

"Yeah?"

"Thank you."

"For what?"

"For being a good guy. For making me feel special. For being able to get past whatever shit went through your head after you were hurt to be the awesome guy you are today. For not getting dead while you were a SEAL. And for agreeing to volunteer at my school."

"You're welcome." There was a lot more he could've said, but he figured the simple answer said it all.

On his way home ten minutes later, Cooper couldn't hold back the grin. He realized that for the first time in a long time, he was happy. He was horny, but happy. Knowing he was in for long weeks of cold showers and masturbating while wishing he was with Kiera, he still grinned. It would be worth it. *She* would be worth it.

## CHAPTER 7

"When are you coming back down?" Cooper asked Tex as he sat in his car outside the Riverton School for the Deaf. He'd learned that if he turned his hearing aid up all the way, he could use the phone without the teleprompter. Sometimes it was easier to go ahead and use the translation service, but when he spoke with his friends, and of course Kiera, he liked being able to talk to them directly rather than read their words on the screen.

He and the former SEAL had hit if off when he'd visited two months ago, and they'd kept in touch since then. They'd had a couple long conversations about how hard it was to acclimate into civilian after that of a Special Forces operative for so long. Tex had a lot of good tips that had made Cooper really

87

think about his own life and finally come to terms with the shift it'd taken.

But for the last month, they'd been calling to simply shoot the shit. Cooper genuinely liked Tex and they'd made tentative plans for him to visit again. It felt good that Tex wanted to come out specifically to see him. He knew Tex was friends with Wolf and the other SEALs that worked with Commander Hurt, but to hear the other man specifically say he wanted to spend time with him, made Cooper feel as if Tex truly was a friend and wasn't just doing Hurt a favor. At some point Cooper wanted to return the favor and go to Virginia to meet Melody and their children, and to bring Kiera with him when he went.

He and Kiera had spent time almost every day together, and he'd never been happier. Tonight was Friday, and after work she was coming over to his place. Tonight was the night.

He'd wooed and courted her for two months. He'd learned a lot about her, just as she'd done with him. He'd learned that if she didn't have coffee first thing in the morning, he shouldn't try to talk to her about anything important. Just as she'd learned he was very much a morning person rather than a night owl.

They'd had a few disagreements—he wouldn't call them arguments—but they'd ended with better knowledge on both their sides of who the other was. All in all, Cooper was more than certain Kiera was the woman he wanted to spend the rest of his life with, and he hoped she felt the same.

Tonight, he wanted to make love with her. Wanted to show her how much he loved her. He knew she was ready, she'd been telling him with the way she clung to him when they made out, the way she begged him to keep going, and how she'd been pouting when he did pull away. He truly hadn't meant to be a tease, but last weekend, when she'd accused him of just that, he realized that the reason for wanting to wait had long been made moot. He knew her, just as she knew him. It was time to stop torturing them both.

Tex's voice brought him out of his daydreaming about Kiera and back to the present.

"Thought I'd come down next week...if that's all right."

"Hell yeah. It's more than all right. Will Melody and the kids be coming with you?"

"Not this time," Tex said with a hint of displeasure in his tone. "And neither she or the other wives are happy about it. Akilah has a thing at school that she doesn't want to miss."

"Are *you* okay missing it?" Cooper asked.

"Yeah. It's a play and Akilah has a tiny bit part. I've seen her do her lines several times and practiced with her. Not only that, but it's being performed two weekends in a row. I'm seeing her tonight, but Melody wants to go to every performance. There's only so much of that I can take," Tex said with a chuckle.

"How long can you stay?"

"Only a few days. Patrick said he'd put together a quick training session with Wolf's team for me, so I can make it tax deductible and my security company can pay for the trip."

"Awesome," Cooper told him. "Glad that'll work out."

"Me too. So I'll be there on Wednesday and will leave on Sunday. That work?"

"Of course. You want to come to the school and hang out for a couple of hours with me on Thursday? I told the principal I'd give presentations to the older classes about the Navy and being a SEAL."

"I don't know sign language," Tex admitted.

"No biggie. I can translate for you."

"Then yeah, it sounds like fun."

"Have you made arrangements for where you'll stay yet?"

"Nope. That was next on my agenda."

"You can stay at my place," Cooper told him. "I'm sure Wolf and the others would also have no problem with you staying with them."

"I appreciate the offer. You sure I won't be in your way?" Tex asked.

"Nope. I'm fairly certain I can stay with Kiera while you're here."

"That going well then?"

"Yeah. I've never met anyone like her. When I'm not with her, I'm thinking about being with her. And when I *am*, I can't imagine being anywhere else."

"Sounds like me and Melody. I'm happy for you, man," Tex told him.

"Thanks. So I'll see you Wednesday. You need a ride from the airport?" Cooper asked.

"Nope. I'll have Wolf pick me up. See you next week."

"Later."

"Bye."

Cooper clicked off the phone and immediately opened his car door. He'd been spending more and more time at the school and loved every minute of it. Not only did he get to see Kiera, he was able to spend time with Frankie and the other kids. He still rotated classrooms when he was there, but he always made sure to stop into her class before he left for the day.

Seeing Frankie's eyes light up when he saw him was almost as good as seeing Kiera's do the same. Almost.

Trying to keep his mind off the upcoming night, Cooper adjusted his dick in his pants and willed it to recede. The last thing he needed was to pop a woody in a classroom. That shit could get him banned for life...and for good reason. Taking deep breaths, he strode to the door of the school. He would stop by the main office and sign in, see where he could be the most useful, then see Kiera. It was going to be a great day.

Kiera couldn't believe what a difference Cooper had made in Frankie's educational and emotional advancement. Since the day he'd begun to volunteer in her classroom, Frankie had gone from being closed-off to the most popular kid in the class. All the other children wanted to sit by him, they vied to partner with him on assignments and he hadn't sat alone in the lunchroom since that day.

He'd also begun to excel in all aspects of the curriculum. His signing was one hundred percent improved, now that he was putting in the effort to learn it. He was reading on the same level as the rest of the kids in the class and his math skills, which were already pretty good, were out of this world. One of Kiera's favorite things about being a teacher was seeing a student make progress, and the progress Frankie was making was remarkable.

The little boy's situation at home was apparently much more stable now that he and his dad had settled in and his mother was out of his life. At the last parent-teacher conference, his father had admitted that his ex had tried to contact Frankie a few times by calling and hoping her son would answer the phone, but luckily the dad had intercepted the calls. Without the toxic influence of his mother, the little boy was blossoming and thriving.

But it wasn't just Frankie who was doing exceptionally well. Cooper himself had apparently gotten the sign language bug and was learning ASL at an amazing rate. He freely signed with the other teachers at the school now and very rarely had to ask Kiera to interpret, or for a sign anymore. He'd showed her an app he'd been using to help teach himself and it was amazing how well it had worked.

Cooper might not have a college degree, but he was smart, very smart, and Kiera felt extremely lucky to be with him. She'd questioned him a lot when they'd first started dating about if he really wanted to be with *her*, an older woman who wasn't exactly Miss America, and he'd reassured her over and over until, one night, he'd actually gotten pissed at her.

It wasn't exactly a fight, but he'd been so frustrated with her lack of self-esteem when it came to their relationship that he told her it was making him feel self-conscious. He'd said that if he didn't want to be with her, he wouldn't. But he was extremely happy for the first time in his life and being with her made him proud, and had made his transition to civilian life easier.

When she'd thought about it, Kiera had realized he was right. She needed to stop asking herself why Cooper was with her and just enjoy it. No one was pointing and laughing when they went out together. But the bottom line was that if it didn't matter between the two of them, to hell with what anyone else thought.

Once she got past her own hurdles with their

ages, the last month had been idyllic...except for his stubborn refusal to have sex. Kiera was starting to get a complex. She'd all but begged him to make love with her the other night and he'd still refused. What guy did that?

It was confusing and frustrating, but it didn't make her want to break up with him. She just wanted to understand what was holding him back. When they'd first starting dating, she'd gotten it. She liked that Cooper wanted to go slow and really get to know each other before consummating their relationship. But now? She was ready. More than ready. She was going to have a serious talk with him tonight and see where his head was at.

The class was currently having their "talk circle." It was an informal time every day for each child to get to tell the others something they had done the night before or just share a story. It helped with their sign language and social skills.

Little Jenny typically told the class what she'd had for dinner the night before, Rebecca liked to talk about the new puppy her family had just gotten. The rest of the class members each had their own quirks and generally Kiera knew what they would talk about. But not Frankie.

The things he talked about ranged from the

mundane to what his mother used to tell him. Kiera would never forget the day he'd opened up—she figured it was because Cooper had been there—about how his mom had told him he got sick and lost his hearing when he was a baby because God made a mistake in letting him be born in the first place and was punishing him.

Kiera had been appalled, and had done her best to reassure him that whatever his mom had said wasn't true. But it wasn't until one of the little girls in the class had innocently told him, "But if you weren't here then we couldn't be friends," that he'd seemed to loosen up. Thank God for the innocence of children.

Today in the talk circle, Frankie wanted to know more about Cooper's time on the SEAL team.

"Can you tell us more about when you had to use your secret signs with your friends?" he asked Cooper through signing. He'd been obsessed with the topic ever since Cooper had first mentioned it.

She and Cooper had talked about the boundaries of what the first-graders should hear about his military career and what they shouldn't, so Kiera had no doubt that Cooper wouldn't tell the children something that would scare them.

When he answered, he signed slowly and

precisely so all the kids could understand him. She was so proud of how far he'd come in his signing ability and confidence.

"One time we were in the jungle and were watching the bad guys. We had to be very quiet so they didn't hear us."

"Like hide and seek?" Frankie interrupted.

"Exactly like that, bud," Cooper signed with a smile. "Anyway, I was lying near one of my buddies and saw a huge snake in the branches above his head. I knew he was scared to death of snakes, so I signaled to him that there was danger above his head. We had no signal for snake. He nodded and signaled back that he understood and was watching the bad guys. I shook my head and tried to tell him again, but he again misunderstood. Finally, I pointed over his head, then made a weird sign for snake, like this…" Cooper demonstrated, using an exaggerated hand movement that looked nothing like the ASL for snake, and all the kids laughed.

"That got through to my friend. He couldn't stand up because the bad guys would've seen him, he couldn't scream because again…bad guys."

"What did he do?" Frankie signed with a big smile on his face.

"He fainted," Cooper told the little boy and the

rest of the kids. "He was so scared, he literally closed his eyes and passed out right there in the jungle in the middle of the job."

Everyone giggled. Kiera loved the sound. Her classroom was typically very quiet, unlike a room with hearing children. But when her kids laughed, it was one of the most joyous sounds she'd ever heard.

"Did the snake get him?" Frankie asked when he'd stopped laughing.

Cooper shook his head. "No. It didn't come anywhere near him. It just slithered away as if my friend wasn't worth his time. Want to know the best part of the story?"

"What?" Frankie impatiently signed.

"From that moment on, my friend's new nickname was Snake."

Once again, all the kids giggled.

Glancing at her watch and seeing it was time for recess, Kiera waved her hands and informed the kids it was time for break. They immediately stood and began to push their chairs back to their desks as they'd been taught. She watched as Frankie went up to Cooper and tugged on his shirt to get his attention.

When he had it, Frankie signed, "I love you."

Her heart melted.

Cooper crouched down on the balls of his feet and returned the sign, pulling Frankie into his arms for a hug.

Just when she thought she couldn't love the man any more, he blew her away with something like this.

Love. Yes, she loved him. Two months was fast, but deep in her heart, she knew Cooper was the real deal.

Frankie pulled away, smiled up at Cooper, then ran toward his cubby to grab his jacket before lining up behind the other kids.

It was her turn to watch the kids at recess; the teachers took turns so they could all get a break during the day. Kiera didn't have the time she wanted to tell, and show, Cooper how much she appreciated him, so she settled for a quick hug while the kids were busy with their jackets and lining up.

She stood on her tiptoes and tugged his head down to put her lips next to his left ear so he'd be sure to hear her. "You are amazing, Cooper Nelson. I can't wait to show you how amazing I think you are tonight."

He squeezed her hips and smiled down at her when she pulled back. "I'll meet you at your place when you get home, sweetheart."

"Okay."

Then he leaned down and put his own lips at her ear. And he blew her mind. "I'd like to change the nature of our relationship tonight...if you're receptive."

Kiera shivered at the promise she heard in his voice. Finally. "Oh, I'm receptive," she told him breathlessly. "*Very* receptive."

They stood there grinning at each other until a tug on her shirt got Kiera's attention. It was Jenny. "It's time for recess," she signed impatiently.

Cooper immediately let go of Kiera and stepped back, putting a respectable distance between them. "I'll see you later," he signed, then winked at her.

He walked to the front of the line of children, who were waiting patiently to be allowed to go outside. He said goodbye to each one, making sure to ruffle their hair or otherwise make them feel special. When he got to Frankie, Cooper lifted his chin in the way he'd taught the little boy the first day they'd met. When he got a chin lift in return, as well as an, "I think Ms. Kiera likes you," signed in return, he chuckled.

"I'm glad. Because I like her too," he told the little boy. Then he put his big hand on the boy's shoulder, gave it a squeeze and was gone.

Kiera took a deep breath and led her class outside to get some fresh air. As was her routine, she walked around the schoolyard as the kids played, rather than standing against the building. She figured it was better to be on the lookout and accessible in case any of the kids needed anything, rather than huddled near the school.

She took a deep breath, then another, and tried to remember what underwear she'd put on that morning. It looked like Cooper was finally making his move...and she couldn't be more thrilled.

## CHAPTER 8

KIERA WAS LATE GETTING HOME. It had been one thing after another at the end of the day. First, Frankie's dad had wanted a word with her when he came to pick up his son to make sure she was aware that his ex was apparently causing trouble. She was harassing him and threatening to have Frankie taken away for good if he didn't allow her to see him.

He'd contacted the police, both here in Riverton and up in Los Angeles where his ex lived, but he wanted to make sure the school knew to be vigilant when it came to his son.

Kiera reassured the man, letting him know how well Frankie had been doing, before another teacher asked for Kiera's opinion about a lesson plan. Then the principal had come in to shoot the shit.

So she'd been an hour and a half late in leaving for home. As she'd expected, Cooper was waiting when she pulled into the parking lot of her apartment. He was leaning against his car, knee bent, the toe of one boot resting on the concrete, his muscular arms crossed on his chest, sunglasses on, his dark hair shining in the late afternoon sun, and Kiera was aroused just by looking at him.

He oozed masculinity and she knew without a doubt that if the boogie man popped out from behind a bush, Cooper would do whatever it took to keep her safe. It was her certainty that he'd do anything for her that made him so attractive. His good looks were merely a bonus.

"Hey," Kiera said as she climbed out of her car from the parking space next to his. "Sorry I'm late."

Without a word, he straightened and stalked toward her. He put his hands on either side of her neck, tilted her neck up, and kissed her. It wasn't long, but it wasn't short either. She gazed up at him and swallowed hard. Cooper was always intense, but tonight he seemed even more so.

"The rest of your day go okay?" he asked softly.

Kiera nodded. "Yours?"

"Fine. You hungry?"

"I could eat," she told him.

Cooper stared down at her for a long moment before saying, "I've waited my whole life for you, Kiera. I didn't know it was you I was waiting for, but now that I've found you, I never want to let you go."

Her stomach doing summersaults, Kiera brought her hands up and rested them on his biceps. "I don't want you to let me go."

"I'll do stuff in the future that pisses you off, I know I will. I'll say stupid shit, and do things that seem insensitive. But I swear to God, I'll never purposely hurt you."

"I know you won't," Kiera said softly. And she did. As she'd gotten to know Cooper, she'd seen firsthand how careful he was with her.

"But I need to say this…"

He paused as if fortifying himself and Kiera tensed. She dug her fingernails into his arms unconsciously. She couldn't imagine what in the world he had to say that had him so nervous.

He looked her right in the eyes and said, "If you let me inside your body, I'm never letting you go. You need to understand that. Even if I piss you off and you tell me to fuck off, I won't. I'll fight with every molecule in my body to keep you. To make you forgive me. If you're not ready for that level of commitment, tell me now and I'll back off. We'll go inside, have dinner, make out like we've been doing and I'll go home. I do not take you giving me your body lightly, Kiera. If you give yourself to me, you're giving yourself to me. Mind, body, and soul. Be sure, sweetheart. Be absolutely certain you want me in your life before we go any further."

"I love you," Kiera blurted out—then closed her eyes in embarrassment.

She hadn't meant to just throw it out there like that. She had wanted to say it when they were in a romantic moment. Deciding that, now that it was out there, she'd go with it, her eyes opened and she started to say more, but she froze at the look on Cooper's face.

He was staring down at her in awe, but his jaw was ticking like it did when he was pissed about something. Losing her nerve, Kiera simply stared up at him.

Several moments passed, which seemed like an eternity to her, and finally he spoke. "I love you too, Kiera. So much, some days I don't think I can go five more minutes without talking to you, seeing you. So much that the thought of you leaving me makes my heart literally hurt."

She moved a hand to his chest, over his heart, and rubbed gently. "Then why do you look mad?"

"I'm not mad," he countered immediately. "Not in the least. I'm trying not to throw you over my shoulder, run to your apartment and break the door down so I can get you in bed faster."

Kiera smiled then, finally understanding why every muscle in his body seemed so tense. "Why don't you?"

At her words, if possible, his body hardened even more. "Because my woman has been working all day and is hungry. I need to feed her."

"Feed me after, Cooper," she told him, moving her hands up his chest to clasp around the back of his neck. She stood on tiptoes and plastered her body to his. "I've been waiting to have you naked in my bed, to have you inside me, for way too long. Make love with me, Cooper. Put out the fire inside me that no one else but you can douse. Please. For the love of God, I need you."

"And you're okay with what I said earlier? That once I sink into your hot little pussy, I'll never let you go?"

"I'm counting on it. I'm giving you my heart free and clear. I know you'll take care of it. Even if you piss me off in the future, I'm not going anywhere. Just as when I do the same to you, I know you'll never storm out of the house and leave me."

Without another word, Cooper moved one arm so it was around her waist and, keeping her plastered to his side, began to walk toward her apartment.

Kiera smiled, knowing she'd gladly let him lead her wherever he wanted to go.

He used her key to open her door and shut it with one foot once they were inside. He took the time to throw the deadbolt, but otherwise didn't pause. He walked them straight to her bedroom and didn't stop until they were both standing next to her bed.

"Strip," he said, not taking his eyes from hers.

Instead of getting irritated at his order, Kiera did as he asked. She first reached back and removed the barrette from her hair, shaking her head as the blonde locks fell around her shoulders. Loving the gasp that came from Cooper's mouth, she grinned.

"God. I haven't seen an inch of your naked skin yet and I'm so hard, I'm about ready to blow just by looking at your hair," Cooper mumbled.

Kiera didn't stop at his words, even though they made her weak in the knees. She toed off her shoes and then unbuttoned and unzipped her slacks. She pushed them over her hips until they pooled at her feet. Somehow taking her pants off first didn't seem as scary as whipping her shirt off over her head.

Cooper had no such hang-ups. The first thing to go was his shirt, he grabbed a fistful of material at the back of his neck and wrenched it up and over his head with one quick jerk.

Faltering at the hard expanse of his chest exposed in all its glory, Kiera paused to admire him.

"Don't stop," Cooper ordered in a hoarse tone.

Remembering what she'd been doing, and why, Kiera decided to get it over with quickly, like removing a Band-Aid. Crossing her hands at her waist, she gripped the material of her blouse and quickly brought it up and over her head.

She stood awkwardly in front of Cooper in nothing but her underwear. Her non-matching cotton underwear. Her panties were leopard print and her bra was white. They weren't anything fancy or seductive. She'd put them on that morning because they were comfortable, not with the thought she'd be wearing them in front of Cooper that night.

Blushing, and trying not to feel self-conscious, Kiera jerked when she felt Cooper's hands on her hips. He pulled her into his own nearly naked body and she shivered in delight when she felt his warm skin against hers.

"You are beautiful," he said reverently, using his thumbs to brush up and down on her sensitive skin.

"My underwear isn't fancy," Kiera said, biting her lip.

"It's you. And I love it. I love you," he said before dipping his head to kiss her.

They kissed for a long time. Surprisingly, with no urgency. Just long, slow swipes of their tongues, lazily caressing and exploring. Kiera could feel Cooper's erection against her stomach and it made her feel sexy and desired. More than anything he could've said, the evidence of his arousal reassured her.

They both pulled back after several moments and Kiera felt Cooper's hands move up her back. He stopped with his fingers on the clasp of her bra and asked, "Okay?"

Everything he did made her fall that much more in love with him. "Yes, please," she said.

Cooper made quick work of releasing the clasp of her bra, and then she stood in front of him in nothing but her panties.

His eyes went from her face to her chest, and Kiera could see his breathing speed up. He took a deep breath and slowly brought his hands up to her breasts. As if she were made of glass, he caressed her, moving his fingers lightly over each throbbing globe. She squirmed as his light touch tickled her.

"Harder, Cooper," she demanded, putting one of her own hands over his and pressing down with a firm touch. "I won't break."

Following her lead, Cooper used more pressure to caress her. Seeing he had the hang of it, Kiera dropped her hands to his hips and pushed her fingers under the waistband of his boxer briefs. She didn't push them down and off, simply enjoyed the intimacy of the moment.

Cooper caressed her breasts and took both nipples between his fingers and rolled them, making them peak even harder than they'd been. Moving slowly, as if asking permission without words, his head lowered. Kiera arched her back, giving him the permission he sought, and sighed in ecstasy when his lips closed around her nipple.

For several moments, he paid homage to her breasts. Licking, nipping, and even sucking on her. At one point, he sucked so hard on the inside curve of her right breast, Kiera wondered if it would leave a mark.

When he lifted his head, examined the mark he'd left, ran a fingertip over it and smiled, Kiera figured he knew what he was doing the entire time and that he'd purposely given her a hickey.

"Having fun?" she asked dryly.

"Loads," he told her.

Deciding it was time to move the show along, Kiera moved her palms down the outside of his thighs, pushing his underwear with them. She kept going until she was kneeling at his feet and his erection was bobbing in her face.

Taking hold of the almost angry-looking appendage, Kiera had a brief moment of worry that he wouldn't fit. He was big...probably not any more so than other six-foot-two man, but she'd never dated anyone his size.

"It'll fit," Cooper murmured, his hands fluttering around her as if he didn't know where he should put them. He settled on placing them on her shoulders and rubbing her collarbone with his thumbs.

Without a word, Kiera took hold of the base of his dick with one hand and braced herself on his thigh with the other. She lowered her head and licked from the bottom to the pulsing tip. He visibly twitched in her grasp, so she did it again.

A drop of precome appeared at the tip of the purple head and she licked it off.

He groaned and his hands tightened on her shoulders.

She licked him again, then without warning, lowered her mouth over him, taking as much of his length in her mouth as she could.

"Oh my God," Cooper swore. "Fuck, that feels good."

Concentrating on making him feel half as good as he made her feel on a daily basis, she wasn't prepared for him to suddenly hook her under her arms and haul her up so she was standing in front of him once again. She felt the wetness from her mouth and his excitement on her belly as he took several deep breaths.

"Why did you stop me?" Kiera asked somewhat shyly. "Was I not doing it right?"

"Not doing it right?" he asked, his eyebrows shooting up in disbelief. "If anything, you were doing it too right. The first time I come with you, I don't want it to be in your mouth. I want to be deep inside you, feeling your own orgasm squeezing my cock as I explode."

"Oh."

"Yeah, oh." Without another word, he stripped her of her undies and encouraged her to lie back on the mattress. He quickly joined her and knelt over her.

"I love your blonde curls," he said, his eyes glued between her legs.

"You don't want me to shave? It seems to be the current fashion."

"Absolutely not," he said quickly, running a hand through the coarse hair between her legs, spreading the wetness from her center up to her clit. "I love you just the way you are."

Kiera spread her legs, giving him access to where she wanted him most, and couldn't help the way her hips tilted up toward him when she felt his dick brush against her. Looking at the difference between her blonde hair and his dark, was the most erotic thing she'd ever seen.

Without a word, he held up a condom he had between his fingers and asked, "You want to do the honors?"

Kiera shook her head. "I've never done that for a man before. I don't want to mess it up."

"There's not much to mess up, sweetheart," Cooper said with a broad grin on his face. "But I understand. I'll teach you some other time. But you should know, now that you're mine, I would really like to feel nothing between us in the future. You gonna be okay with that?"

Kiera nodded. "Yeah. I'm on the pill. More to regulate my periods than for birth control. As long as we're careful and I don't get pregnant, I'd love to feel you inside me without a condom."

He closed his eyes as if her words alone were enough to send him over the edge, then opened them and said, "Just the thought of orgasming inside you and coating you with my come threatens my tightly held control. Spread your legs wider, sweetheart."

She did as he asked, watching as he quickly took care of covering himself. He gripped the base of his cock and shuffled forward on his knees. He ran his tip up and down her slit then said, "I want to lick and suck every inch of your beautiful pussy, but I'm holding on by a thread as it is. The second I taste you, I know I'll lose all control, so I'll have to save that for later. You ready for me, Kiera?"

"Yes. Make me yours, Cooper."

He groaned and pressed into her slightly, the tip of his cock disappearing between her folds as he said, "Fuck."

Kiera could feel her body clenching at his size, trying to keep him out.

"Relax, sweetheart," he murmured, using his thumb to gently caress the bundle of nerves between her thighs.

His touch on her clit made Kiera moan in delight and she opened her legs farther, wanting more of the pleasurable sensation. He pressed in as he continued to use his hand to distract her.

"Cooper," she said, not knowing if she was distressed or super turned on.

"I'm in, sweetheart. Breathe. Take a breath," he said tenderly.

She did as he suggested, and felt him deep inside her. She felt full, extremely full, and was more thankful than she could say for him giving her a moment to adjust to his size.

Kiera looked up at him and saw that he was crouched over her and wasn't moving a muscle.

"I'm sorry," she whispered.

"For what?" he asked.

She wasn't sure. It just felt like she needed to apologize.

"I know you aren't apologizing for being tight. Or because you obviously haven't had a man in quite a while. Or that you need a moment to adjust. Because if you are, I'm gonna be pissed."

Kiera's lips twitched. When he put it like that, it

did sound stupid. She squirmed under him and they both inhaled at the movement.

"Fuck, you feel good," Cooper breathed. "How you doin'?"

"I'm okay. You can move," Kiera told him, not entirely sure she was telling the truth, but it wasn't like they could lie there motionless all night.

Cooper pulled back an inch, then pushed inside her again.

It felt good.

"That felt good," she told him.

He didn't respond, but smiled down at her. He did it again. And again. Each time pulling out farther before pushing back inside her wet heat slowly and carefully. Eventually his easy, careful thrusts weren't enough.

"More," Kiera said firmly. "I'm good now. I need more."

"Then you'll get it. I'll always give you what you need, sweetheart."

His words were sweet, but at the moment, she didn't want sweet. When he pulled out and thrust inside her the next time, Kiera pressed her own hips up, taking him hard.

"Are you sure?" Cooper asked.

"Yes. Fuck me. Please."

And he did. Time ceased to exist. Only Cooper did. He used his hands, cock, and body to make sure she was pleased. And she was.

After the first time she came, Kiera thought that was it, that Cooper would do what he needed in order to make himself come, but he didn't. He merely smiled down at her, brushed his hand over her forehead and hair, and told her that her exploding in his arms, under him, around him, was the most amazing thing he'd ever seen and felt. Then he proceeded to tell her he wanted to see and feel it again.

It wasn't until she'd come a third time that he finally lost control. He put both hands next to her shoulders on the mattress and took what he needed.

Kiera's gaze wandered from his face to where they were connected and back again. Watching him ramp up to the point of no return was sexy as fuck. When he did finally lose it, he pressed himself as far inside her as he could get and held very still. Kiera could feel him throbbing and wished that she could feel his hot come filling her.

His jaw tensed and his eyes closed in ecstasy as he came. Finally, when he'd emptied himself, his eyes opened and the look in them made Kiera inhale sharply.

"You're mine," he declared. "I'm never letting you go."

"Good. I don't want you to," Kiera fired back.

He smiled, then eased himself down onto her, being careful not to crush her. He rolled to his back and pulled her with him. They both groaned when his softening cock slipped out of her body.

"Do you need to take care of the condom?" she asked softly, running her fingers through the hair on his chest.

"In a minute. I'm enjoying this too much to move," he said in a sleepy voice.

"Me too."

"Close your eyes. Relax."

Kiera tried, but when her stomach growled, they both chuckled. "Guess I'm hungrier than I thought," she said sheepishly.

Cooper turned his head and looked her in the eyes. "I've never laughed during sex before."

"Uh, we're not actually having sex at the moment," she informed him.

His smile got wider. "You know what I mean."

She nodded. "Yeah."

"I like it."

"Me too."

Her stomach growled again.

Cooper shook his head in amusement. "Guess we're getting up."

"Look on the bright side," Kiera said. "We can get up, eat, then have the energy to come back here and do that some more."

"Yeah, I could have dessert after we eat. Good plan."

Kiera knew she was blushing, but nodded anyway.

He had pity on her and sat up, pulling her with him. "I'll take care of the condom. Put on my shirt. Nothing else. I'll meet you in the kitchen to help put something together."

"Bossy," Kiera complained without heat.

He leaned down and kissed her hard, then said, "I warned you what would happen if you let me into that hot body of yours."

"You said that I'd be yours, not that you'd turn into a grunting Neanderthal who wants me barefoot and naked in the kitchen."

"Same thing, baby, same thing," he teased. "Tell me you don't want to wear my shirt and I'll back off."

Kiera bit her lip. She totally wanted to wear his shirt. It would smell like him, come down to at least the middle of her thighs, so she'd be completely covered...and there was just something about wearing his clothes that got to her. She wrinkled her nose and refused to answer.

He merely laughed. "Go on, sweetheart. I'll meet you in the kitchen."

"Okay."

"One more thing," Cooper said.

Kiera turned toward him and raised an eyebrow in question.

"Thank you. Thank you for loving me. For trusting me. For letting me in. You won't regret it."

"I know I won't," Kiera told him decisively. Then she kissed him and climbed out of bed. Knowing she was putting on a show for him, she reached down and grabbed his shirt and pulled it over her head. Grinning at him over her shoulder, she walked toward the door of the bedroom, putting a bit of swagger in her step. "After we eat, we can bring the can of whipped cream back here and see what trouble we can get into."

Laughing at the growl that came out of his mouth, Kiera quickly left the room. She'd never been so happy in her life. She was sexually and emotionally satisfied and had a gorgeous former SEAL in her bedroom, soon to be next to her in the kitchen, helping to make them something for dinner. It was funny how life turned out.

# CHAPTER 9

THE REST of the weekend went much like Friday night. Lots of laughter, eating good food, and sex. Lots of sex. If someone had told Kiera she'd one day find a man who was ten years younger than her, couldn't keep his hands and mouth off her, and she'd have so much sex she'd be sore as a result...she would've laughed at them and told them they were insane.

But by the time Sunday had come around, Kiera was delightfully sore. Cooper was...enthusiastic... which she loved and encouraged. As a result, on Monday morning—he'd stayed all weekend and was still there when her alarm went off for work—realizing sex would be uncomfortable for her, he'd gone down on her and given her a morning orgasm that set the tone for the week.

She'd been sated and content in the knowledge her man genuinely enjoyed not only her body, but being with her.

Now, even after less than a week, they'd already settled into a routine. After she woke up, he made her breakfast while she was in the shower. He left at the same time she did in the morning, going back to his place to grab workout clothes and either meet up with Cutter, Patrick's admin assistant, or run along the beach by himself. He'd show up at the school a little before lunch and they'd spend a pleasant twenty minutes or so eating together before she'd go back to her classroom, and Cooper would wander off to spend time in some of the other classes. He'd always make an appearance in Kiera's class before leaving and meeting her back at her apartment when she got home.

They'd fix dinner together, which was awesomely fun, watch some television while she graded papers and made sure her lessons for the next day were in order, then go to bed. Most of the time it was a couple hours before they actually slept, as the time before was spent enjoying each other's bodies.

Kiera hadn't ever been with a man like Cooper. He was attentive, caring, sexy, and most of all, made sure she was happy. Happy with what they were eating for dinner, happy with what they were watching on television, happy with the temperature, and of course, happy while they were intimate.

It wasn't something she was used to, and she realized pretty quickly that she would need to make sure she didn't take advantage of Cooper's attentiveness and desire to please her. He was stubborn and could be bossy, but she truly loved being around him.

Seeing him at school was simply a bonus. Not many women got to hang out with their boyfriends in the middle of the workday.

"How's your day been?" Cooper asked as he took a bite of the sandwich he'd brought to eat for lunch. He'd also packed her a cup of leftover potato soup they'd made for dinner the night before.

"Good. I think Frankie has a girlfriend."

Cooper grinned. "Let me guess...Jenny?"

"Yup. He's obviously been paying attention to you, because today before morning recess, he held her jacket out for her to put her arms through. He's seen you do that for me several times now."

"And what'd Jenny do?"

"She signed thank you, then kissed him on the cheek."

Cooper's smile got bigger. "Hey, there's nothing wrong with trainin' 'em young."

Kiera rolled her eyes, but couldn't hold back the grin on her face. "True. Did you have fun with your friend this morning?"

"Fun might not be the word," Cooper told her. "We met up with Cutter and did suicides on the beach. Tex sure can move fast for a man with only one leg."

"Let me guess, you did your best to keep up with him."

"He can move fast, but not fast enough," Cooper joked.

Kiera chuckled. "You'll both probably need four ice bags tonight. You retired SEALs think you're supermen, but you pay the price after being all macho."

Cooper leaned toward her and put one hand behind her neck, pulling her closer until they were nose to nose. "Newsflash, sweetheart...we *are* supermen."

Kiera giggled and wrinkled her nose. "And oh so modest too."

Chuckling, Cooper kissed her on the nose and sat back. "I'll admit to a twinge or two, but I'm hoping maybe tonight I can get a back rub from my girlfriend."

"I don't know," Kiera said, lifting one eyebrow. "I bet she'll want something in return."

"Oh, I'll give her something all right," Cooper deadpanned.

A snort escaped Kiera before she could hold it back, and she put her hand over her mouth in mortification at the weird sound.

Cooper merely shook his head at her. "Goof."

"You wouldn't have me any other way," she returned. Expecting him to have another witty comeback, she was somewhat surprised when he didn't even smile.

"You're right, I wouldn't. I adore you, Kiera. Don't ever think I take you for granted, because I don't."

"I know. And the feeling's mutual," she told him.

They stared at each other for a long moment before Kiera broke the intense silence. "You about done?"

"Yeah. You mind if Tex and I pop into your class this afternoon once we give our presentation to the older grades?"

Kiera shook her head. "Absolutely not. The kids will love to see you." She'd mentioned to her principal that a friend of Cooper's would be in town and she'd suggested that maybe the two of them could give a short presentation to the older children about the Navy, what it meant to be a SEAL, and how much work it was.

He stood and crumpled his paper bag. He quickly disposed of it and came back to Kiera. She loved how he towered over her, it made her feel feminine, and the way he took her head in both of his hands only added to that feeling. "How about if we come right before recess again? Will that fit into your lesson plans?"

"I can switch some things around. I'll just move the talk circle to then and we'll do our math lesson later."

"Okay. If it's not a problem."

"It's not a problem," she confirmed.

Cooper leaned down and kissed her gently. He'd kissed her a lot of ways in the last week. Hard, soft, passionate, out of control, teasingly...but she loved the way he kissed her while in public. Easy and gently, with a little bit of tongue, and enough banked passion for her to know he *wished* he could take her right then and there, but was restraining himself.

She smiled up at him. "See you later."

"Yes, you will," he told her. He ran one hand over her hair in a gentle caress before turning and heading out of her classroom into the hall.

Kiera sagged back in her chair and blew out a breath. Whew, Cooper Nelson was lethal...and he was all hers.

Two hours later, Kiera made the "applause" sign along with her students. Cooper and Tex had mesmerized the kids. She'd interpreted for Tex, as he didn't know sign language, and had laughed as Cooper and the kids teased him for not knowing even the simplest signs. She appreciated him playing along. The pride her students felt in knowing something the big, strong military man didn't was obvious in their faces, giggles, and puffed-out chests.

She told the kids to get their jackets and to line up for recess and had a quick conversation with Cooper and Tex. "You guys were great. I appreciate you hamming up your lack of communication skills with the kids, Tex."

"No problem, darlin'. And I wasn't hamming it up. They definitely know more than me when it comes to ASL." He turned to Cooper. "And since when did you get so damn fluent?"

Cooper laughed. "Since I've been here every day

for the last two months. And I've been studying at home. And I have the app. And Kiera practices with me, and—"

"Okay, okay, I get your point," Tex said. "I'm impressed."

"Me too, if I'm being honest," Cooper said.

"You know, That Frankie boy reminds me of a little girl I know. I'd love to get them together somehow," Tex said.

"Frankie could use some more friends," Kiera said. "Does she live around here?"

Tex shook his head. "No. She's the daughter of a Delta Force soldier I know who lives in Texas."

Kiera's brows drew down. "I'm not sure a friend would work out with her being so far away."

Tex smiled a somewhat secret smile. "You don't know Annie like I do," he said cryptically.

Looking at her watch, Kiera said, "I gotta go. It's my day to monitor recess. I need to get out there."

"Want some company?" Cooper asked.

"Yours? Absolutely. But I won't necessarily be able to talk much. I walk around the playground, making sure all is well with the kids."

"No problem. I won't get in your way. I might like to play with the kids myself. Tex, you in?"

"Oh yeah. Maybe we can interest some of the kids in a game of kick the can or something."

"Kick the can?" Kiera asked in disbelief. "Didn't that game go out of style in the eighties?"

Tex looked a little sheepish. "It's fun, don't knock it."

Kiera giggled. "Whatever. I'll see you guys outside."

Cooper, never letting a chance to kiss her go by, swooped down and touched his lips to her cheek quickly. Kiera caught him winking at Frankie after he did it. She simply smiled. She'd never complain about Cooper kissing her, she was just glad he kept it age-appropriate.

She led her students from the classroom and down the hall to the outside door. Once it was open, they all ran out as if the hounds of hell were after them. Kiera smiled. She remembered feeling exactly the same way when she was young.

The schoolyard was surrounded by a chain-link fence to protect the children. There were a few gates around the property, as the intent wasn't to lock the kids inside, but merely to keep them contained and safe while they were playing. Deaf children couldn't hear horns honking or other signs of nearby dangers.

Kiera began her walk around the area, smiling at a group of kids playing in the dirt, stopping to push a few students on the swings, and warning an older group of children to be careful as they tossed a basketball at each other.

She smiled at Tex and Cooper. They had collected a group of kids, both older and younger, and had split them into two teams. She had no idea what they were playing, but it looked like a mixture of keep away, soccer, and tag. Whatever rules they'd made up were a mystery to her, but since everyone seemed to be having a good time, and running off pent-up energy, it didn't really matter.

Something moved in the corner of her eye and Kiera swung her gaze from her extremely fit boyfriend to whatever it was that had caught her attention. She stared for a long moment, not understanding what she was seeing.

Even before her brain caught up to her eyes, she was moving. Frankie was on the far end of the playground and a woman she'd never seen before was inside the play area. She was average height and slender. Her hair was dark and stringy, hanging limply around her face. Her jaw was set and she looked pissed. Her jeans were tight, but the black T-shirt she was wearing was loose on her frame. She had her hand around Frankie's biceps and was forcing him to walk toward the open gate. A blue, older-model car was idling in the parking lot in the direction the woman was taking Frankie.

A kidnapping from school grounds was every teacher's nightmare—hell, it was every person's nightmare, no matter where it happened. And if she could stop it, or at least get a license plate, she would.

Kiera raced toward Frankie and the mystery woman. She caught up to them just as the woman reached the gate.

"Hey, what are you doing?" Kiera yelled, knowing it was a stupid question because it was obvious what the woman was doing.

She didn't answer, but pushed Frankie through the gap in the fence and started for the car. Kiera followed and got around the woman. She stood in front of her and asked again, "What are you doing?"

"I'm here to take my son to the dentist."

Kiera blinked. "What?" she blurted.

"Frankie is my son. He's coming with me," the lady said, a little more belligerently that time.

"Is this your mother?" Kiera signed to Frankie.

Instead of signing back, he simply nodded.

Okay then. All the things Frankie's dad said

about his ex raced through Kiera's mind. She was a drug addict. She was refused custody of Frankie by the courts. She'd been trying to get ahold of Frankie, but his dad had run interference. This wasn't good.

Kiera quickly glanced back at the playground where she'd last seen Cooper. He was still there, oblivious to what was happening on the far end of the play area. She saw a couple of kids standing on the other side of the fence, staring at her in confusion. They obviously knew it was against the rules to leave the school through the fence. The staff at the school had hammered that home over and over again. All visitors had to come into the school through the main doors and check in. They had to leave the same way.

The woman steered Frankie around Kiera and toward the car once more.

Making a split-second decision, Kiera quickly shot off a quick sign to the children standing in the playground watching them. She wanted to scream out to Cooper and Tex, but didn't want to do anything that would put Frankie in even more danger than she instinctively felt he was already in. Without waiting to see what they'd do, she ran to catch up with the surprisingly fast woman and Frankie.

No one was allowed to take a child from the school that wasn't on an approved person list. They were supposed to go to the main office and check the child out...after the secretary made sure it was permitted. And it was certainly not okay for Frankie's mom to pick him up. Not even close.

She grabbed hold of Frankie's shoulder and tried to wrench his mom's grasp off his bicep, but the other woman held on, squeezing her son's arm even tighter, and punched out at Kiera with her free hand.

Kiera let go of Frankie to protect herself, and felt the air whoosh by her face as his mom's fist barely missed her. By the time she stepped back toward the duo, she'd already opened the back door and had shoved her son inside.

Not knowing what else she was supposed to do, Kiera ran around to the other side of the vehicle and breathed a sigh of relief when the door on the opposite side was unlocked. She slipped inside the car and slammed the door behind her.

*What am I doing? This is insane. I should leave this to the cops. But I can't let her take Frankie. No way.*

She sighed in relief when the man behind the wheel didn't immediately drive off. If she'd yelled for Cooper or his friend he most certainly would have. It might take longer for help to arrive as a result, but every second she could keep the two adults talking was another second Cooper had to get to her and Frankie.

"Get out," the woman snarled at Kiera.

She sat back and crossed her arms over her chest. "No."

"What the fuck?" the man in the driver's seat swore. "You didn't say nothin' about no other woman comin' with us, Twila."

"That's because she's not. Get out," Twila ordered again.

"No," Kiera repeated. "You need me to translate for Frankie." It was stupid, but it was the first thing she thought of.

"He's my son. I don't need you to tell him what I'm sayin'."

"You know sign language?" Kiera asked, already knowing the answer from what Frankie's dad had told her.

"No. But no son of mine is gonna do that sissy talking with his hands. He needs to learn how to read lips and say what he wants."

"We gotta get the fuck outta here," the man snarled.

"Then fucking drive," Twila told him with narrowed eyes.

"I'm not kidnappin' no fucking woman."

"But you'll kidnap a kid?" Kiera asked, knowing she should keep her mouth shut, but she was so appalled at what the man implied, it popped out without thought.

"It ain't kidnapping since it's her own fucking kid."

Kiera was glad Frankie couldn't hear. The man had an obvious love of the word fuck, and that wasn't something Frankie needed to pick up. Using her right hand, she reached over and grabbed Frankie's, giving him moral support as she continued to stall for time.

"Um, the courts would disagree," Kiera told him. "And Frankie isn't *your* kid, so it most definitely is kidnapping since you're driving."

"Just drive slow, we'll shove her ass out when we get to the main road," Twila said.

Kiera's hand tightened on Frankie's. She wasn't getting out of this car without him. No way. She signed the word "run" with her left hand, hoping Frankie saw it as she continued to engage Frankie's mom and the thug behind the wheel.

"Look, whatever you think you're going to do with Frankie isn't going to work, he—"

"What I'm going to do is make sure he learns how

to talk, instead of grunting and using his hands to try to fucking talk. Then he's gonna learn how to read lips. It's much more manly than using his hands."

"Reading lips is extremely difficult," Kiera told Twila. "It can take years for someone to learn how to do that. Frankie needs to learn how to read first, and since he can't hear, he needs to associate the words on a page with something. It's not as easy as it seems." She'd had this argument with a few parents over the years but at the moment, she didn't really care if Twila believed her or not, she only needed to stall.

She noted that they were moving very slowly toward the school's exit. She'd prefer they were stationary while they had their talk, but she'd take slow. *Come on, Cooper. I need you.*

"On second thought, why don't we keep 'er?" the slimy man asked. "We owe money to Bud. Maybe he'd take her. High-class pussy that hasn't fucked every man on the block might appeal to him."

Kiera inhaled. "Are you seriously talking about trading me, a human being, for drugs?"

"No," Twila said immediately, and Kiera relaxed a fraction. But her next words had her gasping in shock. "He's talking about giving you to the leader of a gang so he can pimp you out in exchange for drugs." Twila turned her gaze to the man. "I think she'd probably be more trouble than it'd be worth."

"What about it?" the man asked her, catching her eyes in the rearview mirror. "You gonna be trouble?"

# CHAPTER 10

COOPER LAUGHED as Tex barely missed being hit by the small plastic ball. He had no idea what they were doing, but the kids were having a good time running around after the balls while he and Tex tried to keep them away from them. There weren't any official rules, but not getting hit by a ball seemed to be one. They were also trying to prevent the kids from getting from one end of the field to the other. It seemed to be a mixture of soccer and dodgeball.

All his attention was on the four balls being kicked and thrown around the small area and not on what was going on around him, but when he heard an urgent grunting, he whipped his head up and scanned the area.

There were four children running pell-mell

toward their group playing with the balls. They were all vocalizing their urgency. They weren't screaming or talking, but the noises coming out of their mouths were definitely panicked.

"What the hell?" Tex asked, coming up beside him.

Cooper barely noticed, his attention was on the children's hands.

"They left by the gate."

"Teacher said to get help."

"Teacher signed kidnap."

"They got in a car."

"Help, help, help!"

The signs were being repeated over and over and Cooper almost didn't understand them, they were so frantic. But as soon as he realized what was happening, his eyes searched the playground for Kiera. The last time he'd seen her, she was walking on the far side of the play area near the fence.

"What color car?" Cooper signed as soon as the kids got to him.

"What's going on?" Tex asked urgently.

Without taking his eyes from the children giving him information, he explained, "They say a teacher and a kid were kidnapped. They got in a blue car outside the gate."

"Fuck," Tex swore.

Both men were on the move before anything else was said. Cooper ran backward and quickly signed to the children, "Get everyone inside. Find a teacher and call the police."

As soon as he saw the kids understood him, he turned and sprinted for where the kids had pointed they'd last seen the car.

He couldn't outrun a vehicle, but he had to see if he could catch up enough to read the license plate. He knew it was Kiera in the car. First, she was the only teacher on the playground, and second, if someone had tried to kidnap one of the children, he knew without a doubt she wouldn't just stand by and let it happen.

"Go," Tex said, falling behind. "My leg won't let me go as fast as you, I'm right behind you."

Cooper didn't bother to respond. He just ran faster. He leaped over the four-foot fence as if he was a world-class hurdler—and couldn't believe it when he saw an older-model navy-blue Mustang going only a couple miles an hour toward the exit.

What the hell was the driver doing? If he or she had just kidnapped a kid, and Kiera, they should be driving like a bat out of hell to escape.

Everything inside him became focused on the

car. It was still there. It wasn't too late. If they got out of the parking lot, it would be almost impossible to find...at least quickly. And giving a kidnapper time to hurt Kiera wasn't something he was willing to do. His muscles responded without input from his brain, his SEAL training kicking in.

Seeing the direction the car was going, he ran diagonally across the lot, never taking his eyes off it. Cooper could see two people in the front and two in the backseat, one being a child. He could tell it was Kiera in the car, even from just the back of her head. He'd recognize her anywhere.

The adrenaline surged through his body. No fucking way was anyone going to take away the best thing that had ever happened to him.

Running through his options, Cooper shoved his hand in his pocket. Jackpot. Having his key ring and the tool on it would make entry into the kidnapper's vehicle easy, but everything else was a crap shoot. He knew Tex would be at his back as soon as he caught up. He had no idea how Kiera would react, but he had to think she'd do whatever she could to protect the child. He could take care of the two assholes in the front.

Time slowed as he approached the getaway car from the driver's side. As he got closer, Cooper could see it was Frankie in the backseat with Kiera. His teeth ground together.

No. Just no. No one was going to hurt that little boy. Not on his watch.

He gripped his keys tightly and timed his actions. He had to strike at the perfect time. Too soon and he'd lose the element of surprise and the driver would most likely take off. Too late and the car would turn onto the main road and be gone. No, he had to time this perfectly.

Kiera couldn't believe Frankie's mom and the thug were talking about selling her to a man so he could pimp her out. It was unbelievable. It was ridiculous. It was terrifying. "Am I going to be trouble?" she asked, repeating his question. "Yeah, you bet your ass I am. Look, Twila, you haven't done anything yet. You haven't even left the school premises. Just stop the car and let me and Frankie get out. We won't say anything."

"You think I believe that?" she asked.

"You should. I don't want to be sold so people can have sex with me, and I think your son would truly love a relationship with you that doesn't include being scared for his life. But you won't have that unless you let us out right now."

"Let's dump her ass," the man said. "She talks too much."

"I agree," Twila said, then turned in her seat and pointed at Kiera. "Get out."

"No," Kiera said. "I'm not leaving without Frankie."

Twila fiddled with something in her lap, and the next thing Kiera knew, she was looking down the barrel of a gun. "I said, get out."

Kiera had never even held a gun in her life, let alone looked down the ass end of one. "N-no." she stammered. "You don't want to shoot me in front of your son."

"Why not?" Twila asked, as if she didn't have a care in the world. "It might make him more of a man."

Kiera snorted. "You think making him watch his beloved teacher get shot right in front of him will make him more of a man? It'll probably make him a psychotic mess who will end up killing you when he's in his twenties for making his life a living hell."

"You're a little dramatic," Twila observed.

"And you're a little insane."

The two women glared at each other. Kiera heard

Frankie making distressed noises in the back of his throat, but she refused to look away from the gun. If she only had a few more seconds left on this Earth, she wasn't going to be a coward.

Everything seemed to happen in slow motion after that.

The sound of breaking glass was loud in the small space of the car and Kiera flinched, thinking for a moment Twila had actually pulled the trigger.

The man driving swore and slammed on the brake. Since no one was wearing a seat belt, they all flew forward. Kiera saw an arm reach through the broken driver's side window and pull the man driving out through the small space. But before she could move, Twila had recovered and was reaching into the backseat toward Frankie.

Kiera reacted without thought. She threw herself in front of the little boy and grabbed the handle of his door. As it popped open, she pushed Frankie with all her strength. He flew sideways and she saw his little feet go flying in the air as he landed on his back and butt on the ground outside the vehicle.

She hoped he'd do as she'd told him earlier and run, but Kiera didn't have time to worry about him. Twila was pissed. And was acting like a woman possessed. She hit and clawed every inch of skin she could reach. Kiera turned her head to protect her eyes and did her best to keep Twila from hurting her.

Not able to see what was going on with the driver, only hearing grunts and the sounds of fists landing on bare skin, Kiera got up on her knees and began to fight back. It was awkward with the seat between them, but the thought of Twila overpowering her and getting her hands back on Frankie was enough to fuel Kiera's adrenaline.

After an especially hard punch to the side of her head, Kiera decided to reciprocate. She fisted her hand and swung it at Twila. When she made contact with the woman's face, it hurt, but she did it again, then again. With each strike, Twila would grunt, but then she'd come right back at Kiera.

Kiera hurt. Her hand hurt where she'd been hitting the other woman. Her face and head ached where Twila had landed blows, and she was tiring. She loved that Cooper worked out, but it wasn't the top of her favorite things to do.

Just as she made the decision to back off and get out of the car and haul ass, which she should've done the second she pushed Frankie out, the front door next to Twila opened and a large arm reached into the car.

Twila was hauled out and away from Kiera, and she watched in relief as Tex easily manhandled the other woman into submission. He had one arm around her chest and the other around her neck. Even though she twisted, screamed, and fought against him, she wasn't going anywhere.

"You all right?" Tex asked.

Remembering Frankie for the first time, Kiera didn't answer him, but scooted toward the open side door and quickly stood. "Frankie!" she yelled frantically.

"He's fine," Tex told her. "Ran like the wind back toward the school. Smart kid."

Kiera breathed out a sigh of relief.

"Kiera," a voice said from next to her.

Whirling, and wincing at the pain it caused, she saw Cooper standing next to her. She'd never seen a more welcome sight in all her life. She threw herself at him and sighed in relief when she felt his arms close around her. She rested her cheek against his chest and clutched at the back of his T-shirt.

"Shhhhh, I got you," Cooper murmured. "You're safe."

Kiera was shaking so hard she knew she wouldn't be able to stand if Cooper wasn't holding her up.

"I hear sirens," Tex announced.

Kiera didn't even lift her head. Sirens meant the cops, hopefully. "Where's the driver?" she mumbled.

"Unconscious," Tex told her.

Kiera lifted her head, which felt as if it weighed nine hundred pounds, and looked up at Cooper. He had a trickle of blood coming out of his left ear. She brought a hand up to his face and gently pushed. He allowed it, and she saw he no longer had his hearing aid in. Taking a deep breath, she brought her other hand up between them and signed, "Are you okay? You're bleeding."

"So are you," Cooper said out loud. He traced a line down her cheek and she winced.

"You need to see a doctor about your ear. It's bleeding," Kiera insisted…as much as she could insist through signing.

"He got a lucky shot. As I pulled him out of the car, he punched me in the side of the head. My hearing aid took the brunt of the damage. I'm okay, sweetheart."

"Are you sure?"

"I'm sure."

"Okay." Kiera took him at his word. She wanted to know how he'd gotten in the car so easily, but it would have to wait. She was extremely grateful he'd shown up when he had. She'd hoped she could stall long enough that the students she'd signed to could get help, but she hadn't been positive. They'd been so close to the main road. So close to having Twila succeed. So close to disaster.

But her SEAL had protected her. He'd gotten there in time. Everything else could wait.

## CHAPTER 11

"Frankie, it's your turn in the talk circle," Kiera said gently. "Do you have anything you want to share?"

It had been a week since Frankie's mom had tried to kidnap him, and today was the boy's first day back in school. Kiera herself had taken a few days off, but even though she still had bruises and deep scratches on her face from Twila's fingernails, Kiera refused to stay home.

She wanted to be with her kids. Not only the ones in her class, but all of them. Those who had run to get help, who gave her huge hugs in the hallways, and even the kids she didn't know but who'd made it a point to stop her and tell her they were glad she was all right.

She hadn't set out to be a hero, but when she'd

seen Frankie being hauled away, she'd made the split-second decision to do everything she could to stop the abduction. Not only was it her obligation as a teacher at the school, but it was Frankie. She loved all the kids in her class, but he was special.

He'd reverted back to shades of the person he'd been when he'd first started attending the special school. But Kiera had confidence he'd bounce back quickly.

Without looking up, Frankie slowly signed, "I was scared when my mom came to take me away. But Ms. Kiera was suddenly right there with me. She didn't let me be taken." He looked up then. "I love you."

Kiera's eyes filled with tears and she smiled at the little boy. "Come here," she signed. He got up and came over to her. Kiera pulled him into her lap, put her arm around him, and signed to him, and the rest of the class.

"I love you all. You are special to me. I will always do everything I can to keep you safe."

Frankie turned in her arms and ran a little finger over the worst scratch on her face. It was scabbed over and bruised, but she didn't even feel his gentle touch. "You got hurt."

"So did you," Kiera said, touching his upper arm

gently where she knew he had bruises from the tight grip his mom had on him.

Suddenly, he smiled. A smile so wide she was momentarily blinded. "We used our secret language."

Kiera grinned back at him. "Yes, we did."

"I like it."

"You like to sign?"

He nodded. "I can talk to people without anyone knowing what I am saying. Like you did when you told me to run. Like Cooper and his friends do."

Kiera wanted to laugh and rejoice in the resilience of children, but she needed to get a word of caution in before she did. "It's not nice to talk about people when they don't understand. You don't like it when people talk in front of you and you can't hear what they're saying, do you?"

Frankie shook his head.

"It's the same sort of thing, sweetie. Don't ever be a bully and make fun of people or purposely talk about them when they don't understand."

"But if we need to, like when my mommy stole me, it's okay?"

"Yes, in emergencies, it's okay."

"Okay," he signed, then squirmed to get off her lap.

"Anyone else want to share anything before recess?"

As if she'd said the magic word, all the kids leaped up from their spots on the floor and ran toward their cubbies.

Kiera laughed, knowing that would be their reaction. Remarkably, even though Frankie had been taken from the playground, the other children didn't seem to have any aversion or reluctance to go outside. The adults, however, were another matter.

The principal had made sure all of the gates were locked the very next day and was making plans for even more security. It had been a rude awakening for a school that hadn't ever had any violence directed toward it, but danger was always a threat and should be mitigated as much as possible. He apologized to Kiera for being reactive rather than proactive, but she'd told him he had nothing to be sorry for. No one could've predicted Frankie's mom would've done what she did.

Kiera felt an arm curl around her waist as she stood at her windows watching the kids run around outside. Frankie and the others might be okay with being on the playground, but she was having a harder time.

"Good afternoon, sweetheart," Cooper said into her ear.

Kiera relaxed back into him. "Hey, how'd your meeting with Patrick go?" She turned in his arms and rested her hands on his chest.

"Really good. He listened to my entire presentation, all twenty minutes of it, without a word. I was sweating bullets, thinking he was merely humoring me and he was about to tell me I wasn't qualified, or that it wasn't a good idea."

"And?" Kiera asked when he paused. "What did he say?"

"He said the job was mine as soon as I opened my mouth. Bastard made me go through my entire presentation for nothing."

Kiera grinned up at Cooper. "I'm proud of you."

"Thanks. But don't be proud yet. I haven't even started."

She shook her head. "You've come a really long way, Cooper. You told me yourself that you had no idea what to do when you retired. Now you're learning sign language, really quickly as a matter of fact, and you made your own job as a consultant to the SEALs teaching them that language. It's amazing."

He shrugged. "The longer I thought about it, the

more I realized it was really important for the SEALs to all be on the same page when it came to our signals. I've seen Wolf and his team talk with each other via signals and didn't understand anything they were saying. The same with Tex. When we were playing with the kids that day, I was trying to signal him to go one way and he had no clue what I was trying to say. I know a lot of the teams stay together for a long time, but sometimes they don't. It would be so much easier if the signs everyone used were the same. Especially if we needed backup in the field."

"I love you," she told him.

"I love you too," he returned. "And I have a present for you." He loosened one hand from around her waist and moved it to one of his front pockets. "Hold out your hand."

She did. He placed a plastic device in her palm, and Kiera blinked down at it in confusion. "Uh... thanks...what is it?"

Cooper chuckled. "It's a glass popper."

She nodded in understanding. "Like the one you used?"

"Yup. It fits nicely on a key ring. You never know when having a little device to easily break a car window will come in handy."

"Thank God you had yours in your pocket when you came after us," Kiera mused, still looking down at the lifesaving device in her hand. "It wasn't like he was going to open the door and let you in." She told him something he knew.

Cooper didn't say anything but instead returned his hand to her lower back and pressed her into him. "Move in with me."

Kiera's gaze whipped up to his. "What?"

"Move in with me," he repeated. "We've been living together for the past week or so and dating for the last couple months."

"Are you asking because of what happened?" she asked gently. "Because that was a fluke thing."

"Yes and no," he told her. "When I realized that it was you in the back of that car, I swear my life flashed in front of my eyes in a way it never had before. I've been in tight spots in the past, but nothing had prepared me to come face to face with the reality of my life without you. I'm not an idiot, I know either one of us could be in a car accident and killed tomorrow. We could get sick, a crazed terrorist could blow up an airplane we just happened to be in, or we could die a hundred other ways. But I want to spend as much time with you as possible. I want to hear your laughter before I go to sleep each night and I want your beautiful blue eyes to be the first things I see when I wake up each morning. I think you more than proved you can take care of yourself last week. I just can't imagine not spending the rest of my life with you, and I want the rest of my life to start as soon as possible."

"Yes," Kiera said as soon as he finished speaking.

"Yes?"

"Yes," she repeated. "I'll move in with you. I love you. I've loved being with you every night and morning over the last week. I crave it."

They smiled at each other for a long moment before Cooper said, "I'm going to ask you to marry me, you know."

"Good. I'm going to say yes."

"Tex says he wants us to come to Virginia and visit him and Melody. And he promises that it'll be more laid back than his vacation down here was."

Kiera burst out laughing. She liked Tex. Not only did he help come to her rescue, he was funny and down to earth. And with the stories he told about his wife, she had a feeling she'd like her too. "I'm sure I can get a few days off. It's not like the principal is gonna deny me," she said with a grin.

"I love you, Kiera Hamilton. You scared ten years off my life last week."

"I think they were scared off of me too," she admitted. "Thank you for coming to my rescue. In case I haven't told you yet."

"Only eighty times," Cooper teased.

They heard the kids entering the hallway, coming in from recess.

"Looks like break time is over," Kiera said unnecessarily. "I'll see you at home?"

"Home. I like that," Cooper said. "Yeah, you'll see me at home."

He kissed her quickly before the kids came into the room, then pulled away. He greeted each child as they entered and headed for the door. Kiera watched as he turned in the doorway. He signed "I love you" to her, then turned to Frankie and gave him a small chin lift.

The little boy returned the gesture, grinning from ear to ear.

Kiera smiled, knowing Frankie would be okay. And so would she. Bruises would fade, as would the memories of the week before, but her love for the gentle, badass former SEAL, who by some miracle loved her, would last a lifetime.

Make sure you pick up Cutter's story...*Protecting Dakota*. Find out who the Silver Fox decides is his and how he protects her!

JOIN my Newsletter and find out about sales, free books, contests and new releases before anyone else!! Click HERE

Want to know when my books go on sale? Follow me on Bookbub HERE!

Would you like Susan's Book Protecting Caroline for FREE?
Click HERE

### *Also by Susan Stoker*

## SEAL of Protection Series

*Protecting Caroline*

*Protecting Alabama*

*Protecting Fiona*

*Marrying Caroline (novella)*

*Protecting Summer*

*Protecting Cheyenne*

*Protecting Jessyka*

*Protecting Julie (novella)*

*Protecting Melody*

*Protecting the Future*

*Protecting Kiera (novella)*

*Protecting Dakota*

## SEAL of Protection: Legacy Series

*Securing Caite (Jan 2019)*

*Securing Sidney (May 2019)*

*Securing Piper (Sept 2019)*

*Securing Zoey (TBA)*

*Securing Avery (TBA)*

*Securing Kalee (TBA)*

## Delta Force Heroes Series

*Rescuing Rayne*

*Rescuing Aimee (novella)*

*Rescuing Emily*

*Rescuing Harley*

*Marrying Emily*

*Rescuing Kassie*

*Rescuing Bryn*

*Rescuing Casey*

*Rescuing Sadie*

*Rescuing Wendy*

*Rescuing Mary (Oct 2018)*

*Rescuing Macie (April 2019)*

## Badge of Honor: Texas Heroes Series

*Justice for Mackenzie*

*Justice for Mickie*

*Justice for Corrie*

*Justice for Laine (novella)*

*Shelter for Elizabeth*

*Justice for Boone*

*Shelter for Adeline*

*Shelter for Sophie*

*Justice for Erin*

*Justice for Milena*

*Shelter for Blythe*

*Justice for Hope (Sept 2018)*

*Shelter for Quinn (Feb 2019)*
*Shelter for Koren (June 2019)*
*Shelter for Penelope (Oct 2019)*

## Ace Security Series
*Claiming Grace*
*Claiming Alexis*
*Claiming Bailey*
*Claiming Felicity*

## *Mountain Mercenaries Series*
*Defending Allye (Aug 2018)*
*Defending Chloe (Dec 2018)*
*Defending Morgan (Mar 2019)*
*Defending Harlow (July 2019)*
*Defending Everly (TBA)*
*Defending Zara (TBA)*
*Defending Raven (TBA)*

## Stand Alone
*The Guardian Mist*
*Nature's Rift*
*A Princess for Cale*
*A Moment in Time- A Collection of Short Stories*
*Lambert's Lady*

### *Special Operations Fan Fiction*
http://www.stokeraces.com/kindle-worlds.html

### Beyond Reality Series
*Outback Hearts*

*Flaming Hearts*

*Frozen Hearts*

### Writing as Annie George:
*Stepbrother Virgin (erotic novella)*

# ABOUT THE AUTHOR

*New York Times, USA Today* and *Wall Street Journal* Bestselling Author Susan Stoker has a heart as big as the state of Tennessee where she lives, but this all American girl has also spent the last eighteen years living in Missouri, California, Colorado, Indiana, and Texas. She's married to a retired Army man who now gets to follow *her* around the country.

She debuted her first series in 2014 and quickly followed that up with the SEAL of Protection Series, which solidified her love of writing and creating stories readers can get lost in.

If you enjoyed this book, or any book, please consider leaving a review. It's appreciated by authors more than you'll know.

www.stokeraces.com
susan@stokeraces.com

facebook.com/authorsusanstoker

twitter.com/Susan_Stoker

instagram.com/authorsusanstoker

goodreads.com/SusanStoker

bookbub.com/authors/susan-stoker

amazon.com/author/susanstoker